Feathered Friendship

✷ A Strange Space™ Novella ✷

KATIE SILVERWINGS

Memphis, TN

PEPTALK PRODUCTIONS, LLC

Publisher's Cataloging-in-Publication Data provided by Five Rainbows Cataloging Services

Names: Silverwings, Katie, 1991- author.
Title: Feathered friendship : a Strange Space novella / Katie Silverwings.
Description: Memphis, TN : PepTalk Productions, 2024. | Series: Strange Space adventures, bk. 1.
Identifiers: LCCN 2024906025 (print) | ISBN 978-1-959922-17-9 (paperback) | ISBN 978-1-959922-18-6 (hardcover) | ISBN 978-1-959922-19-3 (ebook) | ISBN 978-1-959922-20-9 (audiobook)
Subjects: LCSH: Healing--Fiction. | Friendship--Fiction. | Extraterrestrial beings--Fiction. |Family--Fiction. | Outer space--Fiction. | Science fiction. | BISAC: FICTION / Science Fiction/ Action & Adventure. | FICTION / Science Fiction / Alien Contact. | FICTION / Friendship. |GSAFD: Science fiction.
Classification: LCC PS3619.I58 F43 2024 (print) | LCC PS3619. I58 (ebook) | DDC 813/.6--dc23.

Published by PepTalk Productions, LLC 2024
Memphis, Tennessee, USA
www.PepTalkProductionsLLC.com

To the Tiger, the Cheesy-Bats, and the two felines who stare over my shoulder while I'm writing.

Your steadfast encouragement is much appreciated!

Books by Katie Silverwings

FEATHERED FRIENDSHIP
✴ A Strange Space™ Novella ✴

CELADON
✴ A Strange Space™ Novel ✴

HOW OCEAN MERLANI STOLE THEIR NAVIGATOR
✴ A Strange Space™ Novel ✴

WARMTH AND DARKNESS
✴ A Strange Space™ Novella ✴

THE GARDEN IN THE DARKNESS
✴ A Strange Space™ Novel ✴

Available now on Amazon and Barnes & Noble and at
www.KatieSilverwings.com

The printing of this edition of *Feathered Friendship* was made possible through the generous support of the members of the Strange Space™ Fan Club, including:

Astral Navigator

Sharon T. Hinton

Space Adventurer (1 Year)

Tabitha

Thank you so much to all of my Fan Club members and supporters! I couldn't do this without you.

To find out more about the Strange Space™ Fan Club and join for free, visit:

www.KatieSilverwings.com/Fan-Club

Characters Appearing in this Story

The following list of characters is divided by species and arranged in order of their appearance in the narrative. Only characters with significant "speaking roles" have been detailed here. All others present are listed as a group for the reader's reference; characters who are mentioned but do not appear are not included.

Humans

Dr. Ariadne Salzar-Newman
She/her. Also known as "Ari" or "Dr. S.". Biology department head, MSS *Venture.* Wife of **Zoë.** Adoptive niece of **Elder Navy.**

Zoë
She/her and they/them. Lead Astral Navigator, MSS *Venture.* Counterpart to **Elder Navy** and spouse of **Dr. Salzar-Newman.**

Hans Freiburg
He/him. Secondary Astral Navigator, MSS *Venture.* Counterpart to **Ciel Yrvi.**

Gunther Hannemann
He/him. Captain, MSS *Venture.*

Other Humans Appearing
Lt. Timms, Julian "Sarge" Potts

Florivans

COBALT MEREDAY

They/them. Also known as "Coby". Provisional Apprentice to **Elder Navy.** Adopted kitten of **Cerulean Mirawynd** and grand-kitten of **Elder Celadon.**

ELDER NAVY IRLEEIM

They/them. Lead Quantum Space Drive Engineer, MSS *Venture.* Counterpart to **Zoë.** Adoptive entile of **Dr. Ariadne Salzar-Newman.** Parent of **Ilvin, Ilrel,** and **Irvai.**

CIEL YRVI

They/them. Also known as "Cici". Secondary QSD Engineer, MSS *Venture.* Counterpart to **Hans Freiburg.**

ELDER CELADON TOREVAL

They/them. Lead QSD Engineer, LSS *Starbright.* Adoptive grandparent of **Cobalt Mereday.**

ILVIN, ILREL, AND IRVAI

They/them. The kittens of **Elder Navy's** third litter.

OTHER FLORIVANS APPEARING

Elder Guirmean, The Eldest of the Council, The Florivan Council of Elders, Cerulean Mirawynd

Budgerigars

SALZAR-NEWMAN'S BERNADETTE OF *VENTURE*
She/her. Also known as "Bernie", "Chirps", and "Bernadette Venture".

SALZAR-NEWMAN'S ALBERT OF *VENTURE*
He/him

GALLWAY'S SHINING RICO
He/him

OTHER BUDGERIGARS OF THE FLOCK
Judith, Archibald, Monica (and others)

CONTENTS

CONTENTS

Feathered Friendship

✶ *A Strange Space™ Novella* ✶

KATIE SILVERWINGS

Part 1: The Scientist

I N A SMALL PRIVATE LABORATORY ON THE STARSHIP MSS *Venture*, a woman sits sorting through images and data on a set of holoscreens. She's dressed in the ship's standard yellow-accented gray sciences department uniform with the knee-length kilt-style skort instead of trousers. A long white lab coat drapes over the top of her uniform, the ship's insignia and her name neatly embroidered over the breast pocket. An especially bright yellow and green bird is perched on top of the woman's head, sleeping with its feet securely gripping the elastic band holding her wild reddish-brown curls up in a looped ponytail.

This is Dr. Ariadne Salzar-Newman, one of the most brilliant xenobiologists to have ever graduated from the Central Academy of Sciences at Teegarden's Star. She's the head of *Venture's* bioscience team, and in her spare time is something of an enthusiast for the Earth species *Melopsittacus undulatus*, more commonly known as the budgerigar, a member of the parakeet family.

One whole wall of the space behind her is arranged with open cages and a wide variety of perches, ropes, and hanging toys. A dozen more budgerigars of various colors are sleeping on and around these perches. The birds have free reign of Dr. Salzar-Newman's personal workroom, and although they're technically supposed to *stay* there, the one currently sleeping on her head often accompanies her wherever she goes. A long weighted bead curtain hangs over the door of the workroom to discourage the rest of the birds from escaping into *Venture's* main biosciences laboratory.

The running joke among the other members of her team is that one day, she's liable to grow feathers herself, for all the affection she has for her birds. They respect her despite this bit of eccentricity—or perhaps in part because they find it endearing.

A wind-chime toned voice from the other side of the bead curtain draws Dr. Salzar-Newman's attention away from her work.

"Dr. S! Are you home?"

"I'm in here, Coby, come on ahead." She spins around in her chair to face the door, disturbing the slumber of the budgerigar perching on her head. It fluffs its feathers out and chirps at her in annoyance before settling back into a comfortable position.

A small adolescent Florivan steps through the bead-covered doorway and into the workroom. This is Cobalt

Mereday, Dr. Salzar-Newman's favorite part-time assistant and protégé. They're a provisional apprentice to *Venture's* senior Quantum Space Drive Engineer, one of the two adult Florivans responsible for moving the ship through the veiled dimension their species calls "Strange Space" with the assistance of their human Astral Navigator counterparts; a form of transit which allows humanity's starships to travel over greater distances than the laws of physics would allow in a reasonable amount of time, but is not without its dangers.

As their public name suggests, under their pattern of tiger-like silver stripes, Cobalt is a brighter blue example of their genderless, asexual, mostly-humanoid species. The hair around their catlike ears and the rest of their head is a mess of silver cowlicks, having once been cut much shorter and now being in the process of growing out. The locks that would otherwise fall into their three golden eyes are secured back with a set of crossed bobby pins that each have a small yellow star on one end. They're dressed in the Nav/Quan department's charcoal gray version of the trouser-cut uniform, tailored to allow all four of their arms and their long silver-tufted prehensile tail to move comfortably. Additionally, they're wearing a small cloth-and-mesh pouch secured on a sash beneath their lower set of arms.

"I didn't expect you so soon, dear—is it morning already?"

"Yes, technically?" Cobalt replies, coming over to her. "You *did* say to come back once I was done helping with the jump shift, and Elder Navy let me out of the second cycle tonight... Have you been in here with the birdies all night again?"

"I suppose I have," Dr. Salzar-Newman says with a bright laugh. "Must have lost track of the time going through those reports Diego gave me earlier. Don't worry, I'll catch some sleep once we're done here. How did your jumps go?"

"It went okay for once, mostly..." All three of Cobalt's eyes shift to one side as they remove the sash and bag and pointedly change the subject. "Elder Navy asked about your bag, by the way, but I didn't know what to tell them except that it was for your research and you said it shouldn't be opened."

"Really? I *know* I spoke to them about this project... perhaps we'll have to discuss it again."

"They said they'd ask you when they see you at breakfast." Cobalt offers the bag to her, holding it carefully. "But that it didn't seem to cause any interference with the jumps, so they'd probably be okay with approving it once they know what you're up to."

"Well, now, that's good news." Dr. Salzar-Newman takes the bag and rolls her chair over to one of the other worktables where she has her incubators and analysis equipment set up. "Now, let's see what you've brought through Quantum Space for me!"

"What *is* in there, anyway, Dr. S.?"

"Ah! Didn't I tell you earlier?"

"You didn't—I was running late for the jump shift, remember?" Cobalt rolls their third eye dramatically while leaving the lower pair still and then smiles. "You just handed it off and said to keep it with me tonight. Now, what is it?"

"Small treasures, dear—I chose two of Judith's clutch for this experiment."

"Eggs?" All three of the young Florivan's golden eyes widen as they look between Dr. Salzar-Newman's excited face and the collection of small birds perched around the room. "You really had me carrying *eggs* through the Strange?"

"I was sure I told you..." Dr. Salzar-Newman clucks her tongue thoughtfully, then brightens again. "But yes, dear, of course! How else could I test for the effects? I love Navy to bits, but you know as well as I do that they were hardly going to let me send a whole *bird* in with you."

"Of course they wouldn't—it's too dangerous. But an egg is a bird too, Dr. S."

"Not yet, Coby! Just the *possibility* of a bird. If there's one thing I've learned hanging around Navy all these years, it's that Quantum Space likes possibilities. Now, let's see what we have here..." Doctor Salzar-Newman carefully opens the layers of mesh padding and removes a small white egg, setting it into a testing apparatus.

Cobalt watches over her shoulder with interest as the equipment scans the egg and shines a light behind it, illuminating the fine red tracings of veins over the yellow mass within and projecting an enhanced image of all of this on the display screen in front of them.

Dr. Salzar-Newman looks back to them with a broad, excited grin. "There we are, Coby, see! One healthy and viable embryo—although we'll have to wait a few more weeks to see how it hatches and if exposure to Quantum Space has affected it at all. I had a *feeling* the shell would be enough to protect it."

"I'm glad the embryo wasn't harmed," says Cobalt, a concerned tone still coloring their voice. The tuft at the end of their tail twitches softly. "That bag of yours would hardly keep the miasmas from getting in..."

"That was the idea behind the mesh design, Coby—and that it'd let them all *out* again when you and Navy brought us back into Normal space. Zoë would never forgive me if I went and exposed myself by accident again, you know."

"Elder Navy wouldn't have been happy either, Dr. S. They wouldn't have let me bring this to you if they thought that it could have hurt you..."

"Both of them worry too much about me, I'd say." Dr. Salzar-Newman chuckles. "Now, now, Coby, don't you start worrying too. I can hear that tone of Navy's in your voice already."

"Yes, ma'am... I'll try not to."

Cobalt, though, has ample reason to be concerned. Direct contact with Quantum Space is *incredibly* harmful to humans. Exposure is known to cause blindness, insanity, and even death in a matter of minutes, depending on the circumstances. This is why a Florivan has to be in the sealed Quantum Space Drive Bay to run the nightly transit cycles while the rest of the ship serves as a safe bubble of "Normal" space; their species is halfway native to the veiled dimension and immune to its effects.

In the course of her career thus far, Dr. Salzar-Newman has been briefly exposed to various amounts of Quantum Space miasmas no fewer than eight times. Her team often attributes her more pronounced eccentricities to this, but as *Venture's* Primary Nav/Quan team can attest, she was mostly the same even before her first significant near-death experience.

"What is this experiment, anyway?" Cobalt asks, tilting their head slightly to one side. "I thought you said you wanted me to help you with research on training birds to serve on starships?"

"I *am* researching that, dear! And what better way for a bird to help than to detect miasma leaks in the case of an emergency?"

From the look on their face, Cobalt is utterly flabbergasted by this thought.

"Now," says Dr. Salzar-Newman, setting the egg into a waiting incubator, "we'll see how one egg does with just the initial half jump cycle's worth of exposure." She takes a second egg out of the pouch to examine it the same way she had the first. "The *other* one will keep riding with you every time you go jumping until it's ready to hatch."

"You *really* might want to make sure Elder Navy's okay with that..."

"Oh, naturally. But they *did* agree to let you assist me and carry the bag, and this experiment is paramount to my research, you see? These two are my proof of concept eggs: I need to know whether exposure can affect the embryos at all, to start, and what happens with a prolonged series of regular exposures."

"You're looking for a specific effect, then?"

"Ideally. It *is* documented that humans who survive longer exposures retain a minor sense of which side of the veil their ship is on, after all—and in rare cases are even able to identify the presence of miasmas almost as well as a Florivan can."

"...Like you do sometimes, then?"

"Precisely! My theory is that a bird could acquire the same ability and be able to patrol a ship with a handler and point out potential miasma leaks and prevent accidents."

Cobalt hesitates for a long moment before nodding slowly. "If you say so, Dr. S... but it might not be good for the birdies."

"That's why we're starting just with these two eggs. If it doesn't work out with them, I'll probably scratch the whole idea and sort out another way to do this." She looks over to Cobalt from the readouts on the egg. "Now, which one do you want for your jumping buddy?"

"You want *me* to pick?"

"You might as well, Coby, you're the one who's going to carry the egg for me." Dr. Salzar-Newman puts the second egg into its incubator and then reaches out a hand and briefly ruffles the young Florivan's mess of silver hair.

Cobalt allows the contact, although their ears twitch with a momentary irritation. Florivans in general are known to be a semi-eusocial and quite tactile-affectionate species. For a number of reasons that they would never openly discuss, Dr. Salzar-Newman is currently the only person in the galaxy whom Cobalt ever allows to touch them, even casually. She's also the only person thus far whom they've come to trust with the full truth of those reasons.

Cobalt becomes very quiet, staring intently at each egg with all three of their golden eyes for some time before gesturing at the second one that was taken out of the bag. "This one, maybe? It doesn't make much difference, but I like this one."

"Any particular reason?"

Cobalt shrugs. "Not really."

"Fair enough!" Dr. Salzar-Newman laughs and stands up from her chair. "Come on, then, help me close this place down for the night so we can both get a bit of rest."

The bird sitting on her head is bothered enough by the abrupt movement now to make a few unhappy chirps and then fly over to the collection of colorful branches where the rest of the flock is sleeping to find a less active place to perch for the night. It might often accompany her around the ship, but it always sleeps in the bird room.

"Elder Navy said to make sure you'd not forgotten to eat dinner if I found you here instead of in your quarters," says Cobalt, busying themself with tidying one of the cluttered workbenches.

"...You know, Coby, I can't remember if I did?" Dr. Salzar-Newman shuts down the holoscreen she'd been staring at before they came in and rests a hand behind her ear in a brief, thoughtful gesture. "We'll just have to drop by the mess to sort out snacks or something on our way."

"That sounds good to me."

As the two of them leave and Dr. Salzar-Newman taps the keypad beside the door to turn off the lights, the two eggs sit silently in their incubators, warm and unaware that they've been chosen for a different destiny altogether from the rest of the clutch they started in.

★

HER FIRST AWARENESS IS THAT SHE EXISTS IN A very small space that no longer fits.

She's cramped up inside the world, barely able to move at all.

Her first *thought* is that it would be nice to have more room.

She strains against the edges of the world.

She discovers both that she has a beak and that this includes a sharp tool right at the end that is perfect for trying to break through the hard walls holding her in.

She makes an excited sound at this realization, then sets to work trying to break through the wall of the world. She doesn't know what to expect on the other side, or even if there *is* an other side to seek out. She tries anyway—the unknown is far better than being cramped up in a world that's too small.

With great effort and exertion, she taps her way into making a small crack. For the first time, she can feel a bit of warm moist air that's *fresh* and *moving* coming into her tiny world through the crack.

I want out, she chirps, now knowing that there is freedom to be had from her confinement. *Let me out!*

Eventually, although she doesn't know how long it takes, she makes the crack big enough that the whole world breaks apart and the walls fall down around her.

She's free now, and in a much bigger place than she's ever known could exist.

She's blind, still, and knows nothing of this bigger world around her. Even so, it's warm and she has a sensation of *softness* underneath her.

Hello! she chirps out, shakily stretching and resting from her efforts, *is anyone there? I've escaped from the small world!*

At first she thinks she's still alone, but then she realizes the strange sounds she hears above her are *voices* coming from somewhere nearby—although she doesn't yet understand what they're saying.

Hello! she chirps again, *Hello!*

I'm free!

Hello!

I'm hungry!

Feed me!

Hello!

★

"There we are! One more perfectly lovely hatchling! Isn't this exciting, Coby?"

"Welcome to the galaxy, little birdie!" Cobalt pauses, looking over the newly emerged bird. "Dr. S.? When will we find out what colors this one is?"

At the moment, like all baby budgerigars, this small pink creature is completely bald and betrays no hint of what their actual appearance will one day be.

"Not too long, dear," Dr. Salzar-Newman tells them, preparing the syringe of nutritious sludge she'll be feeding the little bird. "They'll get their down feathers and open their eyes in ten days or so, and their colored feathers should show up in two or three weeks."

"So we have a while to wait, then."

"We do." She gestures towards the nest box hanging on one corner of the bird room's 'night cage' where a small yellow budgie is peeking out and accepting an offering of food from a bright blue one. "Considering that Judith carries the white-base genes even though *she's* yellow-based herself and Archibald is blue-base, it's entirely possible we'll get a little blue and white bird of some kind. I'll sequence this little one's genome like we did with Albert once they've had something to eat—we'll be able to make a better guess about the feathers then."

"I'm not sure I want to you to tell me," says Cobalt, watching with interest as Dr. Salzar-Newman does her best impression of a mother bird for the hatchling, complete with soft attempts at soothing chirping sounds. "I'd rather let it be a surprise."

She chuckles. "Oh, it'll be a nice surprise regardless—there's several factors that interact to make the different color morphs."

"Okay, then. You'll have to show me your gene charts again." The tone of the young Florivan's voice betrays an enthusiasm almost matching their mentor's for the details of the subject. Their long tufted tail has taken up an equally curious waving motion. "Say, Dr. S.? Don't you think it'd be easier to let Judith and Archibald take care of these chicks like they are the rest of their clutch?"

"Well, easier, yes—but then it would be easier for *me* to lose track of which hatchling was which while they're still featherless like this and too small to give their ID microchips safely. Besides, the rest of the clutch is our control group for this experiment."

"I suppose that makes sense."

"Mind you, Coby," says Dr. Salzar-Newman, grinning up to her assistant, "once this little bird is a bit bigger, *you're* going to be the one making sure they don't go hungry." She pauses, looking over to the incubator in which a slightly larger baby bird is now chirping for attention. "And speaking of hungry budgies, it sounds like Albert's awake. Go ahead and mix up the food like I showed you, and we'll see how you do feeding him once I'm done here."

"Yes, ma'am."

★

TIME PASSES.

Somewhere along the way, her eyes open and she gains a fluffy coating of white feathers on her back.

She's learned by now that she is something called a "bird," like the many birds flying freely around the room belonging to the creature called Doctor-Ess—who is *not* a bird, but something else that is much bigger and has no feathers at all.

She has the impression that one day she'll have nice feathers like the other birds, but for now hers are still grow-ing in. She's not sure yet what color they'll be. Most of the other birds are shades of yellow and blue and green and white and have black stripes across their heads and backs, though, so she's reasonably sure she'll look like one of them. She likes the idea of having more feathers. Feathers are *warm* and seem to be the thing that allows the other birds to fly.

The Doctor-Ess also seems to be her mother, since it's this one that feeds her and cares for her and picks her up to sit her in all the different interesting places that make beeps and whirs. She's not entirely sure why Mother has no feathers or wings and is so much *bigger* than her, but food and care is provided, so mother this creature must be. Her instincts tell her this and she believes them.

There's another tall creature who regularly comes into the room where she and all of the other birds are. Mother calls this creature "Coby," and seems to show them an excited sort of parental affection too. She wonders if that makes the Coby creature her sibling, although they're hardly a bird themself. They're only a bit smaller than Mother, and hardly the same sort of a creature—they're bright blue and silver instead of shades of pale brown, and have two extra limbs, a *tail*, and a third eye, to start. While the Coby still doesn't have any feathers, at least they're a similar color to some of the birds.

She's beginning to understand the language of the other birds—although they don't say much that interests her, past simple things about food and flying and how pretty this or that thing is. She likes the sounds Mother and the Coby use, though, and is starting to be able to understand what their sounds are as words even if she doesn't understand all of the concepts behind those words.

What she likes best right now, though, is that whenever the Coby comes to the side of her warm translucent nest box and peers in with their three large golden eyes, it means that it is time for her to be fed. She's decided that's reason enough to want to keep the Coby as part of her flock, since their presence is a sign of food. She always makes sure to chirp happily at them as thanks for this.

As a growing bird, after all, she's *always* hungry.

★

"How is Bernadette today, Dr. S.?" Cobalt asks, immediately going over to the pair of incubator boxes where the two baby birds who hatched from the eggs they carried into Quantum Space reside. They have a marked fondness for the younger of the hatchlings, possibly because hers was the egg they kept with them for the entire time the baby bird within it was growing.

As soon as Cobalt comes within view of this younger hatchling, the little bird starts chirping excitedly and shakily wiggling closer to the side where the young Florivan is looking in at her.

"She's developing well, Coby," says Dr. Salzar-Newman, joining them at the incubators and gesturing to the hatchling. "See? She has more pinfeathers today."

"She's turning into a very *spiky* little bird." Cobalt holds back a giggle.

"She *does* have a lot of pinfeathers, doesn't she?" Dr. Salzar-Newman reaches a hand in now to gently rub through and help the little bird preen some of her new feathers, particularly the ones at the top of the head where the hatchling's beak can't reach. "Don't worry, they'll lose all of the sheathes and become proper feathers once Bernie grows a bit more."

"Is she going to learn to talk like Rico does?"

"Eventually, Coby, at least that's the plan—although like I've said before, what Rico does is just imitating words he's heard as a flock signal. He doesn't really understand what more than a handful of them mean... and Bernie here's still just a baby. She won't be able to learn anything for the experiments until she's fledged."

"Right. Of course."

Dr. Salzar-Newman turns her attention to Cobalt now, ruffling the mess of silver hair behind their large cat-like ears for a moment with her clean hand. The young Florivan accepts the brief affectionate contact almost as happily as the hatchling had.

"So, how was your first shift back helping Ciel?" Dr. Salzar-Newman asks, going over to the cabinet where all of her baby-bird-feeding supplies are kept.

"It was... okay." Cobalt's eyes are still on the hatchling, but cast downwards a touch as they answer.

"Only okay?"

"...I had to spend most of it sitting with Lt. Freiburg in Nav instead."

"Same problem as usual?"

"...Yeah."

"I see. Are you feeling better now? I hadn't heard much of anything from Navy this morning—just that you'd come in after the shift and curled up in your nest without saying anything."

"I'm *fine*, I just..." Cobalt's tail swishes reluctantly. "I sort of overslept and missed seeing everyone this morning, but I don't think Ciel's told them what happened yet."

"Ah. I had to come down here early and tend to the birds, so if anything was discussed over breakfast, I missed it." Dr. Salzar-Newman holds out a cup with a small syringe sitting in it to Cobalt and gives them a reassuring smile. "Here. Help me give our little birdies their lunch, and then we can have some tea and you can talk about it if you want to before we get started with the other work we have waiting. Okay?"

Cobalt looks up to her for a few moments and then takes the cup and syringe with a hesitant nod.

"Okay."

★

By the time most of the feathers all over her body have grown out, it is clear she is a blue and white sort of a bird. Her coloring is a bit lighter than the Coby's smooth featherless skin, but she still takes the similar colors as a sign that they must truly be siblings.

She also comes to understand that she's been given a name.

She is a "Bernadette," which seems to be a very big name for such a small bird as her, but she likes it because it's *hers*. Mother also calls her "Bernie" a lot of the time, which she assumes is a sign of affection like the way the Coby's proper name seems to be "Cobalt." The similarity of the names is another sign of sibling-hood, in her mind—none of the *other* birds are ever called something other than their proper names, after all.

Therefore, as far as Bernadette is concerned, the Coby is *hers* and *family* just like Mother is.

The other thing Bernadette learns as she grows is that she's somehow just not like the other birds who fly around in the world she knows. She *understands* the things the tall people say, and she wants so badly to talk to them and ask them all sorts of things, but neither her Coby nor Mother seems to understand her chirps at all.

Bernadette finds this incredibly frustrating.

Her odd-looking sibling is often the one taking her out of the nest box and feeding her, now that she's not a helpless scraggly baby anymore. Her Coby's long sets of four fingers aren't as warm as Mother's five-fingered hands are, but they're always gentle and make sure to help her with all of her pinfeathers in the places where she can't reach easily. She's especially grateful for the help with the ones on top of her head—those itch *terribly* when they're ready to lose the waxy sheathes keeping the fully-grown feather safe.

"Now, Bernadette," her Coby says, setting her into the weighing box again, "Doctor S. says you're going to be able to start learning to fly like the other budgies soon. Are you excited about that?"

Even though they don't seem to believe that she understands and wants to carry on the conversation, her Coby does always keep a running one-sided dialogue with her. It's part of why she likes them so much.

Bernadette chirps brightly in response.

She's very much looking forward to having wings that work—although she's not sure *how* it works, exactly. She's been watching the other birds carefully, though. There seems to be a scientific principle at work to keep them aloft, but she hasn't worked it out yet. She wants to be able to ask her Coby how flying works and many other things like that, since they seem to know so much about the world.

She's determined that as soon as she's able to fly, she's going to make the great trek across the open space of the world to meet the old green and yellow bird called "Rico" who can make the most tall-creature sounds of anyone in the flock. Ideally, she'd find a way to make Rico come to *her* sooner, but when he isn't accompanying Mother to the place beyond the bead curtain at the edge of the world, he never seems to fly near Bernadette's nest-box. At times, she almost thinks Rico and the rest of the adult birds are making a point of avoiding coming near her.

Still, it's a quest which Bernadette is eager to undertake. She wants to be able to talk to her sibling almost as much as she wants to be able to fly.

"I thought so," says her Coby. "Albert will have to go first, though, I think. He's almost a week older than you, so he *should* have his flight feathers ready and fledge first."

"Albert" is the name belonging to another young bird who lives in the nest-box next to Bernadette's. He is yellow and loud and somewhat annoying. He does try to talk to her on occasion, but he's only vaguely a better conversationalist than the rest of the birds in the room.

Bernadette has a burning desire now to be able to fly before Albert can, just to show the pompous little floof that she's just as good at being a bird as anyone could ask.

Her Coby finishes whatever they're doing to make the usual set of beeping sounds, then picks her up and holds her towards the nest-box where Albert is sitting and staring at her.

"Do you want to say hello to your brother before I put you back in your nest?"

She chirps at her Coby—meaning to say *no*—but they seem to misunderstand and hold her close so she and Albert can interact.

Hello, Albert. I guess.

Silly not-bird! You have silly stripes!

Isn't it sillier that you don't have them, Albert?

Very silly!

You're the silly one, Albert. I don't see why my Coby thinks you're my brother.

They're not a bird either, silly! No wings!

Bernadette musters all of her strength to hop back up onto her Coby's hand with a pointed chirp and turn her tail feathers towards Albert.

Thankfully, her Coby seems to get the message this time.

"You know, Bernadette," her Coby says, bringing her up close and stroking her chest-feathers a few times before they set her back into her own nest-box. "I get the feeling sometimes that you don't like Albert."

Albert doesn't like me, she wants to say, but it still comes out as chirps that her sibling doesn't understand.

The first time she was introduced to the yellow bird, he'd said that she didn't smell like a proper bird and she therefore couldn't *be* a bird.

There weren't really any grounds for her to want to be friends with him after that.

Albert had told her that she seemed more like her Coby than a proper bird too, although he just kept laughing at her every time she tried to ask him to explain what that *meant*. This was the point where Bernadette decided that the idea of Albert having been one of her siblings at any point in time was ridiculous. If it weren't for the occasional "conversations" she was encouraged to have with the yellow annoyance, she would be happy to ignore the fact that he existed at all.

What she wants now, more than anything, is to be able to fly and talk to the tall people and ride on her Coby's shoulder to leave the confines of the world of birds like they do and see for herself the bigger world that must be waiting outside.

★

"ALL RIGHT, NOW, COBY, IF YOU LOOK AT THE metabolic rate charts on that holoscreen and read off the numbers to me so I can enter them into the system, that's our first step for today."

"Which holoscreen, Dr. S?"

"The one on my pocket-com, dear—I left it on the counter by Bernie's nest-box."

Cobalt walks over and lays their hand on the small silver device, pausing for a few moments to greet the little blue and white bird who's so happily begun chirping at them for attention.

"You mean this one?" they ask, holding the pocket-com up. "You'll have to unlock it, the holoscreen's not project-ing."

Dr. Salzar-Newman turns to look at them and raises an eyebrow. "No, dear, I left it out—I can see it in your hand from here. Are you okay?"

"I..." Cobalt looks down at the device and waves one of their hands through the air around it. The tactile feedback field responds with a mild hum at the point where their fingers meet the holoscreen interface. "Oh. There it is. I'm sorry, Dr. S... I didn't notice."

Dr. Salzar-Newman stops what she's doing and comes over, setting a hand gently on the young Florivan's shoulder and looking carefully at their three golden eyes. "It's that kind of a day, then? You should have told me earlier, Coby. How many doses?"

"...Three," Cobalt replies, hesitating again. "It's not *that* bad... I can see a bit of a shimmer now if I squint. Here." They offer the pocket-com to her, looking away.

She takes it, and then sighs. "You *know* I'm not upset with you, right? We've talked about this. I just need to know if you can't see what we're working on so I can give you something else to do until the side effects wear off."

"I know. It's fine, really. I honestly didn't realize that the screen was out... it's my own fault for being—"

Cobalt is interrupted by a loud chirping.

Bernadette has, for the first time in her life, managed to get her whole body up out of the nest-box and shakily perched on the side of the rim. She chirps even louder, waving her wings excitedly.

"Easy, Bernadette! I see you! Good job!" Cobalt turns to her, whatever they were discussing all but forgotten in the excitement. They take the triumphant little bird up in their upper pair of hands and hold her out to their mentor, grinning broadly. "I think she's trying to talk to us again."

"I wouldn't be surprised if she is." Dr. Salzar-Newman chuckles and gives her young assistant a brief pat behind the ears. "I think she was offended that we were both standing here and *not* giving her food. But this is progress!" She holds out a hand and gives the small blue and white bird a pat on the head too.

Bernadette chirps happily again and waves her wings, hopping up to perch shakily on Cobalt's wrist.

"You know, Cobalt, once she starts flying, Bernie's going to be one of those birds who escapes all the time and gets me in trouble. I just *know* she is." Dr. Salzar-Newman laughs again.

"I'll keep her out of trouble, Dr. S., don't worry." Cobalt helps the small bird up to a comfortable place sitting on their shoulder.

Bernadette is immediately distracted with the bits of silver softness that are now within reach, carefully scooting on her unsteady feet until she's half hidden under the longest portion of Cobalt's hair.

"You know, Coby, I think she's imprinted on you?"

"Birds do that too, then?"

"Mm. Different than the way y'all do, a bit, at least if Navy's been honest the times I've asked them to compare it. Bernie thinks we're her family, because when she was a hatchling I did her mother's job—her instincts would say that 'the one who feeds me is my parent', you know."

"I see. So a little bit like us, then, really... that's why I never questioned that Cerulean was my Nida when I was little, at least..."

"Well, yes, I suppose." Dr. Salzar-Newman nods. "Come

on, then, you can sit with me while I enter these things and keep Bernie out of trouble, since she's decided to be an explorer today—and when you can see the screens again, I'll put you back to work." She smirks brightly. "Unless you want to go through and clean the bird cages a second time today instead?"

"Oh no, I don't mind waiting."

"Thought so."

★

Part 2: The Bird

Iт's AN EXCITING DAY FOR BERNADETTE WHEN A new tall person comes into the bird room for the first time in her life. The newcomer is a slightly taller, inky-blue version of her Coby with much longer hair that's pulled away from their face in a series of intertwined braids with a shimmery piece of sheer pinkish ribbon woven in at the back.

The shimmery ribbon immediately catches her attention as something she'd like to inspect more closely.

"Now, what did you want to show me, Mereday?" the new person asks, following her Coby in from the bigger world's beaded portal.

Bernadette carefully gauges her sibling's position in space, stretches her wings, and hops off of her perch on the edge of her clear nest-box. Landing securely on the cool white surface below, she excitedly hops across the table to greet them. She hasn't quite mastered flying yet, although all of her feathers have grown in. For the moment, hopping is sufficient. Her Coby is coming over to see *her* first like they always do, after all.

She chirps happily when she gets close enough and her sibling reaches out with their long silver-tufted tail to offer her a new perch so they can bring her closer to their hands and pick her up.

"Coby! Morning!" Bernadette adds into her chirps. She still hasn't managed to go all the way across the room to talk to Rico and learn all of his vocabulary of imitated tall-people sounds, but these two words she's got down perfectly. It helps, she thinks, that unlike the other birds, she actually knows what the sounds *mean* even before someone tries to teach them to her. 'Coby,' of course, is her sibling's name; 'Morning' is the first part of the day and a greeting for one's flock members when they appear.

So far, Bernadette is proud to have mastered a grand total of twenty words. She's doubly proud because currently, Albert can only mimic *one*. Even if the yellow annoyance did manage to fly first, he can't begin to challenge her vocabulary.

"Good morning to you too, Bernadette!" her Coby says, rewarding her for her efforts with a stalk of millet once she's taken her usual place on their shoulder. "This is Elder Navy—I told you about them, remember?"

Bernadette tilts her head to one side and then chirps at the bigger version of her Coby. She does her best to make the chirps come across as a hello-and-I-am-happy-to-meet-you-person-called-Navy sort of statement. She's heard her Coby and Mother talk about a person with that name before—she thinks now that this *must* be the person who belongs to the name. Certain of that, Bernadette focuses her eyes on them carefully as she bobs her head and tries her tall-person words again.

"Morning! Nay-vee!"

'Navy', the name of the new Coby-like person, is now word number twenty-one.

"Very good, Bernadette!" Her Coby happily looks over to the new person. "See, Elder Navy? I told you she was smart. She's barely even learning to fly yet and she's already started picking up words just like your kittens do."

"I see, Mereday, I see." Navy nods solemnly. "She's a very nice bird. And *this* is what came out of that egg Ari had you carrying around in the Strange with us for weeks on end?"

Bernadette isn't sure what she thinks of Navy yet. After Mother and her sibling, this is only the third of the tall people she's met. She knows from her Coby's talks with her and with Mother that there are many other tall people in the big home called *Venture* that lies beyond the door to the world of birds, but she's yet to get to see any of that for herself.

"She is! Albert's around somewhere over there with the other budgies, if you want to meet him too. He's the one who only went in with me that first time—he's not as talkative, though. I've barely gotten him to say his name."

Navy shakes their head. "Ari's *lucky* I let her get away with this experiment at all."

"I don't see what's so wrong with it, since we were being

careful... and Bernadette doesn't seem to have suffered any ill effects."

"That you can *see*, Mereday. I still don't like the idea of exposing *anything* to the Strange if we don't have to." Navy sighs, shaking their head again. "I'm not looking forward to trying to explain all of this to the rest of the Council the next time we meet as it is."

"...Yes, Elder." Her Coby's voice shifts to something less excited. "Dr. S. said she wasn't going to do any more runs of experiments until she's sure Bernadette and Albert will be able to pass the other tests we're setting up, anyway. And for that, they have to learn the call words and signals... so it'll be a few months, really."

Navy is quiet for a moment, then tilts their head to one side. "You're really interested in all of this, aren't you, Mereday?"

"...Yes, Elder. At least... I... I like working with Dr. S— and the birds too..."

"Birds! Bernadette-is-a-good-budgie!" Bernadette chirps, trying to show off for her sibling's proof of how good she's getting at repeating the phrases they and Mother want her to learn to say.

"Yes, Bernadette," says her Coby, catching just the edge of a smile. "You're a good budgie—see? That's what I mean. She picked that one up in two days."

"She'll be just like Rico and never stop talking all of her adorable bird nonsense, at this rate," says Navy, their tone finally softening a bit. "This little bird seems to be fond of you, Mereday."

"Dr. S. says she's taken a bird-imprint on me," her Coby responds, absently helping her with one of the few remaining pinfeathers on the top of her head. "But Bernadette is a good little friend, either way."

Navy dramatically lays one of their four hands over their face. "You're going to end up just like Ari letting this bird ride around on your shoulder all the time, aren't you?"

"Oh, really, now, Navy!" says Mother, appearing out of the doorway and coming over to join the three of them, "What's so odd about that? Bernie's going to be a *working* bird, hopefully! She'll need to be socialized to not get stressed out by the rest of the ship."

"Morning! Doctor-S! Morning!" Bernadette calls to her, bobbing her head excitedly. "Bernadette-is-a-good-budgie!"

"Yes, sweetheart! You're a very good budgie!" Mother laughs brightly and offers a hand to her. "Good morning! How's my Bernie today?"

Bernadette flaps her wings and hops the short distance to reach it, nuzzling happily against Mother's cheek when given the chance. She then looks up to the green and yellow bird who often accompanies Mother when she leaves the world of birds and chirps a few happy good morning things at him too. This is the closest she's ever been to Rico. Usually he flies off to join the flock as soon as Mother comes near her.

The old bird looks down at her from his perch in Mother's hair and chirps back, although not with the sort of conversational chirps he uses with the rest of the flock. It's more of a hello-and-I-see-you-still-exist sort of chirp, coming from him.

Terse as it is, Bernadette takes this as a good sign.

Hello! she chirps again, tilting her head to one side at him. *I will learn to fly soon! When I can, will you teach me your songs so I can talk to my Coby and Mother and Navy?*

Fly! Fly and sing! Rico fluffs out the feathers on his chest and flaps his wings. "Howdy-Stranger! Rico-is-a-pretty-bird-pretty-bird!"

Bernadette marvels at the performance. As Rico flies off to join the rest of the birds, she decides to take his response as a promise.

"Oh, dear," says Navy, "the birds are gossiping about you again, Ari."

"More likely," Mother laughs, "they're gossiping about the fruit I brought down for them all from hydroponics."

"You're still *involved* in that, you know." Navy swishes their tail pointedly. "It counts."

"Heh, so I am. Here, Bernie, go back to Coby now, I need my hands to make your breakfast." Mother holds her out where she can flutter back triumphantly onto her Coby's shoulder.

Navy shakes their head again. "Ari, you spoil these birds almost as badly as you do my kittens."

"What can I say? I like seeing my feathered children happy and well-fed just as much as my step-kittens. Now, be a dear and help us get their breakfast in order before the budgies all get too excited and try to get in the way? We can discuss the parameters I'm thinking for Albert and Bernadette's tests after I get the flock fed."

"...You *really* invited me to come in early because you wanted two extra pairs of hands to help you with all this, didn't you?"

"It's a perk, yes!" Mother grins. "Besides, you know you like my birds."

"I like them best now that I'm not living with any of

them."

"You're never going to let me live down the time Monica made a nest in your closet, are you?"

"I forgive, Ariadne, but I have a long memory."

"All right, then, *Elder*, if you would *please* help me with this, I promise you won't have to wait as long."

"Don't worry, Bernadette," whispers her Coby as the other two tall people go over to do whatever it is they're doing with the contents of the large bag Mother was carrying, "They're actually best friends—they just chirp at each other a lot, that's all."

"I heard that, Mereday!" calls Navy from across the room.

Bernadette decides this must mean that the tall person named Navy is part of her flock too.

"It's *true*, though, Navy, isn't it?" asks Mother, halfway between laughing and serious. "Or are we back to being something else?"

"We're *family*, Ariadne—but that doesn't mean you're not the most confounding human I've ever met all the same."

"Ha!" says Mother, giving Navy an affectionate nudge much like Bernadette has seen the birds in the flock do with each other, "and you're still the most oddly *serious* Florivan I've ever come across. That's why we're friends, isn't it?"

"Naturally."

★

OBALT IS BUSY COLLATING DATA BETWEEN TWO of the old-fashioned solid-screen data pads Dr. Salzar-Newman has left for them to enter into the computer database for one of the biosciences department's major projects.

The little budgerigar called Bernadette, now old enough to be able to fly confidently around the room, has just returned to sitting on Cobalt's shoulder and overseeing everything they do. She's spent most of the day pestering the old bird called Rico, repeating words back and forth with him and following him every time he tried to fly to a different perch.

Cobalt has a habit of doing most of their work in a chair in the bird room, as it's not as eerily quiet as the main biosciences laboratory is when all of the human staff members have left for the evening. The birds are always chirping and flying around the room, giving it a genial background noise level that the young Florivan seems to find comforting.

"Okay, so that's all of the gene variants on this one... now where's—ah!" Cobalt snaps the fingers of their left hands. "Right. Lt. Ramirez' notes need to be collated and added into the system too. I must have forgotten to pick those up."

Bernadette chirps and turns her head to one side, looking between the screens.

Cobalt pushes their rolling chair back from the desk and stands, giving Bernadette a little pat on the head. "Hold on, Bernadette. You can come with me, but I'll get in trouble if you fly off my shoulder, so stay put, okay?"

"Bernadette-is-a-good-budgie!"

"Yes, that's right! You are."

With Bernadette perched on their shoulder, Cobalt steps through the bead curtain separating the bird room from the rest of the biosciences lab.

"Coby! Big!" Bernadette chirps while they're walking over to get the notes downloaded onto another data pad. "World-is-a-big-place-for-a-little-bird!"

"Yes, it is—say! That's a new phrase! Did you pick that up while you were pestering Rico earlier?"

"Rico-is-a-pretty-bird-pretty-bird!"

Cobalt laughs. "I'll take that as a yes."

Once they've finished downloading the Lieutenant's notes onto their data pad, Cobalt starts back towards the bird room door.

"Thank you for not trying to fly off, Bernadette. I'll be sure to tell Dr. S. how good you were. Maybe she'll let me start showing you around the ship sooner than we—"

The young Florivan's voice suddenly breaks as they pause mid-sentence, dropping the data pads onto the floor. Their ears swivel around erratically, as if seeking out the source of a particularly distressing sound. They close all three eyes and freeze where they stand, all while one of their lower hands frantically searches for something carried within the pockets of their jacket.

"Coby?" Bernadette flutters her wings and preens a few strands of their silver hair.

Cobalt takes a long deep breath and opens their eyes. One of their free hands comes up to stroke the small blue and white bird's feathers.

"It's nothing, Bernadette, I..." They pause for a moment to withdraw a small flask from their pocket and take a measured sip. "I just hear and see things that aren't there sometimes, that's all. It'll go away again soon."

"Birds-in-the-bird-room-all's-well-with-the-galaxy!"

"Rico taught you that one too?" Cobalt slips the flask back into their pocket and bends down to pick up their dropped data pads. "...Yeah, all's well now. Come on, let's get back to work. I think I'm going to turn in early once this is done."

★

SEVERAL DAYS AFTER HER FIRST BRIEF FORAY into the wonders of the outside world, Bernadette is allowed to ride around with Coby everywhere they go. She's ecstatic about this, particularly because the big world is full of all sorts of exciting and interesting places to explore.

She's learned every imitation sound Rico had to teach her, but now that she's able to constantly listen in to the conversations of the tall people around her, she knows she'll be able to pick up even more of *their* words too.

She's come to understand that Mother is something called a human, while Coby and the others like them are Florivans—different *species* of tall people who come from different *planets*, which are big round worlds with people and birds like her living on some of them. Today, she's learned that her home isn't a world in itself but a *starship* called MSS *Venture* which travels between these planets.

Bernadette has also begun to suspect that it's not normal at all for a bird like her to be able to understand the conversations around them or do more than imitate words and associate them with things like food and tricks. Whenever she tries to assemble her own sentences and actually carry on a conversation, unfortunately, Mother seems to think that she's just very *good* at imitating things.

Her Coby, though, tries to keep a running dialogue with her and is always happy to explain what's going on. For example, currently she's riding on their shoulder to visit a place called the "Nav Closet"—which is, as far as Bernadette understands, the place where Astral Navigators are stored—and they're doing their best to explain to her why the three miniature Florivans she met this morning aren't allowed to visit the bird room.

"So, from what Dr. S. has told me," Coby continues, "before the kittens started shedding their fur, Ilvin's initial 'shiny things are for us to collect and make nests with' phase included wanting to borrow some of Rico's feathers while he was still wearing them."

"Shiny-things?"

"Oh, you'd have to ask Ilvin about that. It all went on long before Elder Navy took me for their apprentice. My *guess* would be that they spend too much time around Dr. S. and liked the bright colors." Coby almost giggles. "Anyway, the flock's still a bit frightened of the kittens, even though they've mostly grown out of it. I mean, Ilvin seemed pretty keen not to give *you* a reason to peck them earlier, so the feeling's pretty mutual from what I can see."

The three smaller Florivans, Bernadette has learned, are the offspring of the full-sized one called Navy. The kittens are currently only a smidgen larger than her, and covered in soft silver fur that's started to shed off in patches on their ears and around their shoulders. From what she understands, eventually the three of them will lose the rest of their fur and grow to be somewhat Coby-sized— and then they'll be sent to a *different* starship to serve an apprenticeship like the one her sibling is in now.

Bernadette hasn't put together yet all the details about why that is or what Coby actually *does* in the nighttime when they're not in the bird room. She knows it has something to do with moving the ship forward to wherever it's going in space, but the rest of what she's overheard makes very little sense to her.

"Ah!" says Coby, turning a corner and going through one of the automatic doors, "Here we are, Bernadette! That big room out there is *Venture's* Command Bridge... and back here is the Nav Closet."

The few humans who are busy at the different consoles in the Bridge area and happen to notice their presence either nod or wave briefly to Coby. They wave back, and then walk through the second little door. It slips shut behind them.

Bernadette has already decided that she doesn't like automatic doors. They don't want to obey her when she tries to use them on her own—not that she'd be allowed out of the bird room without her sibling as an escort, of course.

"Good evening, Zoë! I hope we're not interrupting you?"

"Good evening, Cobalt! No, no, I'm just pulling charts for the jump cycle, I can spare a few minutes." The tall, pale human with the neatly wound up black hair turns the swiveling chair around towards the door. "And... does Ari *know* you've borrowed one of her birds?"

"She's being habituated to the bustle of the ship so we can have her ready for the tests," Coby answers.

"Ah, right. So which of the ones from the big experiment is this, then?"

"This is Bernadette! Albert isn't all that interested in leaving the bird room, unfortunately."

Bernadette, of course, is perfectly happy that the yellow nuisance had declined Coby's offer to come along with the two of them today. She's quite glad he's decided he'd rather be part of the bird room flock than go exploring.

"Ah," says Zoë, "so *this* is the Bernie I've heard so much about. Good evening to you too, then, little bird."

Bernadette bobs her head and chirps politely. They've not met in person before, but she knows that this *has* to be the Zoë who Mother talks about so fondly all the time—the one who is her reason for being friends with Navy. From what Bernadette has gathered while listening to Mother and Coby talk, Zoë is a special sort of human who is mostly a 'she' like Mother, but some days is also a 'they' like Coby. Bernadette doesn't know enough about humans in general yet to understand any of that, really, but she knows this is a person who is *very* important to Mother and therefore is a member of her flock.

"So, is she handling being out of the bird room well, then?"

"Better than Dr. S. expected, actually!" Coby grins

proudly, then makes a sort of sheepish gesture with their long tufted tail. "But since I have to go meet up with Elder Navy now and I don't have time to take her back to the bird room *and* get to the Drive Bay on time... I was wondering if Bernadette could maybe sit with you for a while instead?"

"You really *are* spending too much time with Ari, aren't you?" Zoë chuckles warmly. "Fine, the bird can stay, but if she makes a mess in here—"

"—She's the best-behaved budgerigar in the galaxy, Zoë," Coby protests. "Aren't you, Bernadette? You'll be good for Zoë and not bother her while she's working, right?"

"Bernadette-is-a-good-budgie," she says, bobbing her head again. Since it seems she'll be staying here, she takes the opportunity to fly up from Coby's shoulder to the top of the high-backed chair Zoë is sitting in. It's a nice perch, particularly since it lets her see all of the interesting things on the screens that are set up around the room.

"Ah, right... you and Ari *did* say that this one talks, didn't you?"

"She listens, too!" Coby says. "I'm pretty sure she actually understands when we're talking to her—Dr. S. says that's more wishful thinking and anthropomorphizing on my part than actual fact, though."

"Is that so?" Zoë looks up and tilts her head to one side at Bernadette. "Well, then, bird, just try to be quiet while I'm working, will you?"

Bernadette works through in her mind the long list of words she's figured out how to say and the sounds that make them and then settles on a response.

"Bernadette-is-a-quiet-budgie!"

Zoë looks back to Coby. "Remind me, will you, to tell my wife that this pet project of hers is starting to be a bit too creepy for my liking. Or did *you* teach her to say that?"

"No, and she's *not* creepy." Coby twitches their ears in mild irritation before shooting Bernadette a pointed smile. "But she *is* very smart—I'm pretty sure she's figured out how sentences work."

Zoë sighs. "Just get going, Cobalt. You know how Navy feels about tardiness—and remember, the kittens are going to be with you tonight, so try not to let any of them get misplaced."

"...You don't really think I'd let that happen, do you?" Coby's voice takes on an almost hurt tone, but only for a moment.

"No, Cobalt," says Zoë, reassuringly and half laughing. "It's more just that I know there's three of them and one of you and even *I* can't keep those fuzzy little scamps out of trouble half the time when Navy leaves them up here with me."

Bernadette, sitting on the back of the chair, looks down to her sibling with a flutter of her feathers. "Coby-goes-to-work-now!"

"Yes, Bernadette." Coby waves to her and turns toward the door. "I'll be back later to pick you up."

With that, Bernadette is left alone in the room full of diagrams and displays and additional holoscreens surrounding the central chair.

"Now, so you just sit there and stay out of my way—okay, Bernie?" Zoë pauses for a moment, then sets her hand over her face and makes a sound that's halfway between a sigh and a laugh. "And now I'm talking to the birds. Maybe *I'm* the one who's been around Ari too long."

Bernadette does as she's been asked and remains silent. She's far too interested in looking around at all of the things in the room and trying to figure out what the lines and words and drawings all mean.

Zoë reaches up and pulls down the little bar on the headset she's wearing so that it's in line with her mouth. "Navy, I just sent Cobalt down to you. If you hear anything weird tonight, it's because they've left Ari's little mad science project up here with me."

From one side of the headset near Zoë's ear, Bernadette hears bell-like laughter. Curious, she repositions herself more on that side of the chair-back so she can hear better.

"Oh? Well, the kittens liked little Bernadette, for what it's worth—they've been chattering about her all afternoon." Navy laughs again. *"Planning on teaching your little feathered daughter to read star charts, then?"*

"Oooh, don't you start on me, Irleeim." Zoë chuckles for a moment, and then focuses her attention on one of her computer interfaces.

A few minutes later, Coby joins the other Florivan voice *wherever* they are and Zoë and Navy coordinate a pair of long involved checklists of things like "door seals" and "intercom connections" and "quantum analysis computer interfaces." Bernadette listens intently from her perch on the back of the chair, all the while still trying to piece together what's going on.

"All right, Navy, that's the last of our checks. Prepare to make our first jump of the night on my mark." Zoë taps another series of buttons on the control pad on the chair's armrest and then speaks again in a more formal voice.

"All hands, prepare for jump to Quantum Space. All Nav/Quan safety protocols are now in effect. Jumping in thirty seconds."

At the same time, Bernadette hears Navy's voice in the headset counting backwards. When they reach one, the voice falls silent. At the same time, she feels the familiar but inexplicable sensation of all of her feathers being rustled by some unseen static charge rushing like a wind across her and the entire ship.

Bernadette is used to this sensation; she feels it regularly during the ship's arbitrary 'night' period, usually every hour or two. None of the other birds ever seemed bothered by it if they felt it, though, and she's generally assumed that they don't. She *had* once asked Albert if his feathers were affected by whatever the odd static feeling is—but this had proven to be a mistake, because ever since he's teased her mercilessly about being a silly not-bird who feels things that aren't there.

One of the best parts about being allowed out of the bird room, of course, is that Albert isn't here to tease her. She ruffles out all of her feathers and starts preening the static out of them.

"Jump to Quantum Space confirmed, Zoë; do you have coordinates ready for us?"

"Yes, just a moment." Zoë pulls a little holoscreen and stylus out of the armrest and taps it. "Your Primal is still Kapteyn, and your local origin is 30 by 38F and 1F," she says, and then rattles off a list of other labeled points and numbers.

"All right. We've got our bearings now. Destination?"

"Do you want a full jump or a half-distance?"

"Full, I think. We're running smoothly so far."

"Full it is, then! Jump-out point's 32 by 34B and 5. Sound good?"

"Sounds good, Zoë. We'll call when we reach it."

After this, there's silence over Zoë's headset. She turns her chair around and starts tapping through the various lists on her displays.

Bernadette watches eagerly, trying to put together what all of this means.

★

SEVERAL HOURS PASS, WITH PERIODIC CHECK-INS from Navy and Coby and exchanges of odd lists of coordinate numbers as the only interruptions to Zoë's quiet chart-reading routine.

Bernadette keeps herself occupied with feather-preening and looking at the various charts and displays to try to figure out what they mean. She's gotten relatively good at reading the language of the tall people recently, since she spends so much of her time keeping Coby company as they're working. They've even started to read bits of things out loud to her, when she's shown the right sort of interest.

Zoë's displays are a bit too advanced for Bernadette, though. All of the words and numbers and charts seem to run together with no hint of their context, no matter how many times she tries to read them. She wants to try and ask what it all means—and what Coby and Navy are *doing*, wherever they are, for that matter—but she's promised to be quiet, so her questions will have to wait.

Some time after the fourth exchange of coordinate numbers, while Zoë is once again silently contemplating the information on her display screens, a light chime sounds from the little work chamber's door.

"Enter," Zoë calls, still distracted by her charts and numbers.

"Hey, Zoë—I brought coffee." Mother walks in, carrying a tall covered mug like the ones she often brings into the bird room when she's working.

"Ari, you're a wonder!" Zoë turns the chair around. "Please tell me you've come to pick up your feathered daughter as well?"

"Ah! Hello, Bernie!" Mother comes over and places the steaming mug in Zoë's hand so she can properly reach up and give Bernadette's feathers a soft stroking, "I was wondering where you were."

Bernadette would normally greet Mother with a lot of exuberant chirping, but since Zoë has asked her to be quiet, she settles for quietly flapping her wings and bobbing her head.

Mother giggles, then looks down to Zoë. "So, love, what do you think of her?"

"Well..." Zoë glances up to Bernadette briefly and then chuckles. "Let's just say I'm glad she's not as loud and messy as the rest of your birds."

"Oh? That's odd. Bernie's usually pretty talkative."

"Bernadette-is-a-quiet-bird," Bernadette informs her

in as quiet a voice as she can manage, bobbing her head happily.

"Well, she *was* being quiet, until you came in." Zoë looks up to Mother, with a fond smile and a tone that's only halfway serious. "Please, Ari, if you're going to talk to the bird, take her away? You know I'm working—and *you're* distraction enough on your own."

"I know, I know." Mother smiles and then looks back up to Bernadette and pats the perching-spot on her shoulder. "Come on, Bernie, let's leave Zoë alone now so she can work."

Bernadette reluctantly flutters over to her shoulder and then looks back to Zoë and dips her head and wings.

"Thank-you-Zoë!" she says, still trying not to chirp it out too loudly.

Zoë looks like she's about to say something, and then holds up a hand at some voice from her headset in a wait-a-moment gesture. "All right, location confirmed as 37 by 34E and 9. Proceed with jump back to Normal space in thirty seconds."

Mother stands quietly and watches with Bernadette as Zoë follows her routine of tapping buttons on her armrest's holoscreen and making a similar announcement over the ship's intercom. That done, Zoë deftly tucks the stylus back behind her ear.

Bernadette shivers again as the static feeling begins to ruffle the edges of all of her feathers at once. She's never felt so much of it at one time before. She feels a similar shiver run through Mother's shoulder, even through the thick layers of uniform she wears.

Mother shuts her eyes and sets a hand on the door

frame. When Bernadette looks toward it, she sees the pale fingers gripping tightly, as if Mother *needs* a perch like that to hold her up.

"Return to Normal space confirmed," says Zoë, still focused on her headset and screens. "If everything's okay down there, we'll set for the next one in five minutes. I just need to let the quantum analysis compile and the ship markers update—looks like we've got more folks in the area to keep an eye on, now that we're approaching Sol."

The static now past, Bernadette sets about rearranging her feathers. She stops after a moment to nudge Mother's cheek instead, because she's never seen the pinkness drain away from it like this before. She wasn't aware before now that Mother could feel the static too—or that it could have such a strong effect on her.

Mother still has her eyes closed tight. Bernadette nudges her cheek again and makes some soft chirps to try to reassure her without being too loud.

Zoë looks over to them now, her face shifting to a more concerned expression. "Ari? You okay?"

"Yeah," Mother says, finally opening her eyes. She slowly removes her hand from the door frame and rubs both of them together. "It was just a bit... *sharper*... than usual that time."

Zoë slides her chair over and sets her hands on Mother's. "You got distracted and forgot to eat your dinner again, didn't you?"

Mother is silent, as if contemplating the question, then lets out a single half-hearted laugh. "Possibly. I don't remember... I'll get a snack or something on my way back to the lab."

"Promise?" One of Zoë's hands reaches up to gently touch Mother's cheek for a moment.

"Promise."

"Good." Zoë looks up at Bernadette and chuckles. "Bernie? Hold her to that for me, will you?"

"Bernadette-is-a-good-budgie!" she replies, "Time-for-snick-snacks-little-birdies!"

"It's downright eerie how she acts like she understands us, you know?" Zoë says to Mother, removing her hands and returning to her work.

"Eerie?" Mother laughs, sounding like herself again. "Who, this sweet little thing?"

"Yes. *Eerie.*" Zoë glances back pointedly at Bernadette. "I'd bet anything she's just pretending to be a normal bird."

"Bernadette-is-not-a-normal-bird?" Bernadette asks, looking up to Mother and tilting her head to one side. Considering how many times she's been informed that she isn't a proper bird at all—at least by Albert—it's confusing that Zoë seems to think the same thing.

Mother is silent for a moment, looking at Bernadette closely. "You know, Zoë?" she says at last, "I think I have some tests I need to do. I'll see you later?"

"If you're still awake when we have the mid-shift break, yeah. I'll come find you."

"Great." Mother's usual enthusiastic mood has returned in full. "Come on, Bernadette, we have work to do too!"

★

"Okay, Bernie! Let's see if you're just very clever at imitating... or if Coby and Zoë are on to something." Dr. Salzar-Newman absently munches on one of the strawberries she'd picked up from the crew mess on her way back to her workroom. She points to Bernadette with the stem. "Who are you, little bird?"

"Bernadette-is-a-good-budgie!" The bird sitting on the table in front of Dr. Salzar-Newman bobs her head happily. Bernadette takes a nibble off of the remaining bit of strawberry on the stem before adding, "Bernadette-is-a-Bernadette!"

Dr. Salzar-Newman looks at the bird for a moment and makes a note on the holoscreen beside her. "Okay. Good answer... Now, how about me? Who am I?"

The bird is silent for a moment, then flutters her wings excitedly. "Dr.-S.-is-a-good-human! Dr.-S.-is-Mother!"

Dr. Salzar-Newman's eyes widen, and then she chuckles. "That's sweet, Bernie." She offers the bird the stem of another strawberry while she makes a few more notes, and then gestures to the bowl of strawberries the two of them are sharing. "What about these?"

"Strawberries! Time-for-snick-snacks-little-birdies!" The bird pauses and tilts her head to one side before adding, "Time-for-snick-snacks-for-Mother!"

Dr. Salzar-Newman laughs. "Well, you've certainly got a good memory, Bernie. Yes, yes, Zoë and Navy are always fussing at me for getting distracted with my work..."

"Navy-is-a-good-Florivan!" Bernadette says unprompted with a cheerful bobbing of her head. "Zoë-is-a-good-human! Navy-and-Zoë-loves-Mother!"

"I know they do." Dr. Salzar-Newman smiles, although the tone of her voice says that she's equal parts baffled and fascinated. "I didn't know that *you* knew that, though."

"Bernadette-loves-Mother!" the bird adds.

"Aww, Bernie." She shakes her head. "That's sweet too, but all of this is still stuff you might have reasonably been expected to learn how to say. There's *precident* to rearranging phrases and responding to keywords, at least—but I've never encountered a budgie as young as you who could do that before, though, and certainly not to this extent."

The little blue and white bird tilts her head as if waiting for another question to answer.

Dr. Salzar-Newman makes another note or two on her datapad and then taps her stylus to her lips. "Okay, what else can we try? Let's see... Ah! I know. Who's my assistant?

Can you tell me about them?"

The bird chirps happily and wags her tailfeathers the same way she does every morning when the person in question enters the bird room. "Assistant-is-Coby! Coby-is-a-good-Florivan! Bernadette-is-blue-like-Coby! Coby-is-sibling-of-Bernadette!"

The Doctor laughs at this description and adds some more notes to her growing collection. "So you *certainly* have a sense of object permanence and identities of the people you've met. That's incredible, Bernie."

"Bernadette-is-a-smart-budgie!" Bernadette flaps her wings excitedly and lightly fluffs out her feathers for a moment.

"Yes, you are. Let's see... Here's a challenge for you: how about our home? Where do we all live, Bernie?"

"Birds-in-the-bird-room-all's-well-with-the-galaxy!" The bird preens a few feathers on her wing before looking back up at Dr. Salzar-Newman and tilting her head slightly to one side again. "Bernadette-in-the-bird-room! Bernadette-in-*Venture*!"

"Ooh... okay, and what is *Venture*?"

"*Venture*-is-home!" Bernadette adds in an imitation of the whistle the ship's intercom system makes before an announcement. "*Venture*-is-shiny-starship!"

"So it is!" Dr. Salzar-Newman claps lightly for a moment or two. "I *know* I've never taught you that specifically... or has Coby been telling you things?"

"Coby-talks-to-Bernadette! Coby-talks-to-Mother!"

"So you might be able to piece together information from what you've heard us say, too? Incredible! I can't wait until Coby comes off the jump shift to show them this—and to apologize for not paying attention to what they've been telling me about you."

Bernadette bobs her head happily.

"Okay, Bernie, tell me something else." Dr. Salzar-Newman smiles softly and picks up another strawberry to nibble on. "Your choice."

The bird is silent for a long time. Finally, she chirps and pointedly stretches her wing towards the perches on the other side of the room where the rest of Dr. Salzar-Newman's budgerigar flock is going about their business.

"Albert-is-annoying-yellow-bird!"

"*Bernie*!" Dr. Salzar-Newman is startled enough that she almost chokes on her strawberry. "Now, who in the *stars* taught you to say that?"

"Bernadette-taught-Bernadette!" the little bird replies. She fluffs out her head-feathers and flutters her wings for a moment before holding one wing out towards the perches again. "Albert-is-annoying-yellow-bird!"

The yellow budgerigar named Albert doesn't seem to recognize that he's been insulted, even though from where he's perching with the other budgies on the other side of the small room he doubtless could have heard her. He doesn't so much as look Bernadette's way.

"Incredible." Dr. Salzar-Newman shakes her head. "Although I'll admit, Bernie, I don't quite understand why he annoys you." She taps through the menus on her datapad and then sends off a message.

Bernadette folds her wings back, seemingly content to have said all she might possibly have to say about the subject. She hops up onto the rim of the bowl of strawberries and looks down at the datapad. She tilts her head to one side as if trying to read the contents of the screen.

A few moments later, a pinging sound alerts Dr. Salzar-Newman to a new message. She reads it and smiles before looking back to the curious little bird perching on the rim of the bowl. "Okay, Bernie, I have another test in mind for you. Are you up for a bit of a challenge?"

"Bernadette-is-a-smart-budgie!"

Dr. Salzar-Newman laughs and offers the bird her hand. "I'll take that as a yes. Come on, we'll be going back to my quarters for this."

Bernadette hops up onto the hand with a happy chirp.

★

For the first time, Bernadette finds herself in the space that Mother's flock occupies aboard *Venture*. It's bigger than the bird room, certainly, with doors along the internal hallway near the entrance on either side which lead to three smaller sleeping-nest rooms and a lavatory. The central sitting area features a curving orange-upholstered couch and two matching chairs around a low table. The walls are covered in cabinet doors, hanging pictures, and shelves full of books and interesting objects. There's also a wide viewport on the far wall of the open space—although at the moment this is covered tightly by a shutter.

Bernadette enjoys herself flying around the space and perching in different places while Mother is busy setting up a teapot and cups on the small table in the middle of the sitting area. There are a lot of interesting things to see, after all, between the collected objects on the shelves and all of the different nooks and crannies for storage in the walls.

A few minutes after Mother finally sits down in one of the chairs and pulls out her note-taking screen, a chime sounds at the door.

"Come in," calls Mother.

A pair of new people enter, both wearing the same sort of dark gray uniforms that Navy and Zoë do, although with one blue stripe apiece instead of two along the collars. One of them is a dark brown human with no hair on his head but a long curly mass of the stuff hanging down from his face. He stands about a head shorter than the lighter-than-a-bird-blue Florivan with shoulder-length silver hair who accompanies him.

"Good evening," Mother says, waving to the new arrivals. "Thanks for letting me borrow you for a bit on your night off."

"Not a bother at all, Dr. S." The human chuckles warmly. "You saved me from getting dragged into a poker game with Cici's buddies from ship's operations again, actually."

"Which he *enjoys* when he comes with me, mind you, and only protests because he's terrible at bluffing." The Florivan nudges the human playfully with one of their upper elbows while both of them are taking seats on the couch.

"Oh, is that so?" Mother giggles, then pours a cup of steaming liquid from the pot for each of the visitors to match her own. "I'll admit my ignorance, there—cards have always been more Zoë and Navy's pastime than mine. Poker's something different from what those two play with the Captain and Dr. Yoshida, isn't it?"

"Bridge is a different sort of a game entirely," the human answers, "and it's far too complicated for my taste."

"So, Dr. S.," says the Florivan, waving their tail curiously, "you said you needed some extra eyes looking at one of your experiments?"

"Ah, yes, I did." Mother holds out her hand in front of her. "Bernie? Come over here so I can introduce you."

Bernadette flits down from her perch at the top of the bookcase and lands gracefully on Mother's hand. She chirps happily and then turns herself so she's facing the two interesting people Mother seems to have invited to meet her.

"Why am I not surprised that the experiment you wanted help with has *feathers*?" The human shakes his head in a good-natured way.

"Ooh! Such a lovely color, though—it reminds me a bit of one of my older sibs." The Florivan smiles appreciatively and then turns their third eye up to Mother, keeping their lower two on Bernadette. "Is this Cobalt's bird, then? Or do you have another experiment going on that no one's told me about?"

"Yes, it is. This is Bernadette. Say hello to the Lieutenants, Bernie—they're going to help me with the rest of the test I was doing with you earlier."

Bernadette fluffs her feathers and stretches out her wings, then bobs her head happily at the two of them. "Hello! Bernadette-is-a-good-budgie!"

"Hello, Bernadette!" says the Florivan.

"Nice to meet you, little bird," says the human. "Cobalt's certainly talked about you enough."

Bernadette bobs her head again to each of them. "Nice-to-meet-you!" she echoes.

"So, what exactly is this test we're helping with?" asks the Florivan with a curious twitch of their ears.

"Well," says Mother, taking on the same tone of voice she uses when she's explaining some task or other to Coby, "Bernie here met Zoë for the first time earlier tonight... who's pointed out something about her behavior to me that Cobalt had mentioned too, but that I hadn't seriously considered before. I've already run some preliminary tests with her, but I'd like to try it again with someone *else* she hasn't met before today to see if what I'm suspecting is true."

"And what exactly *are* you suspecting, Dr. S.?" asks the human, raising one of his eyebrows.

"Oh, you'll see once we get started. I wouldn't want to prime your impressions any more than I have to." Mother smiles and gestures towards the two visitors. "Okay, Bernie, first question: Can you tell me who these lovely people are?"

Bernadette considers the question and tilts her head to take a closer look at the two people sitting on the couch. She thinks back through all the things Mother and Coby have said about the other people who live outside the bird room in the bigger world of the starship called *Venture*. After a few moments, she's pieced together the information she needs and found the right phrases in her vocabulary of imitated words to make answers.

"Lieutenant-Ciel-is-a-good-Florivan!" Bernadette happily bobs her head as she makes her declaration. "Ciel-is-

Quantum-Space-Drive-Engineer! Ciel-is-star-doctor!" She stretches one of her wings in the direction of the other person on the couch. "Lieutenant-Freiburg-is-a-good-human! Freiburg-is-Astral-Navigator!"

The two young officers look between Bernadette and Mother with matching stunned expressions.

"If you brought us here to impress us with the phrases you're teaching your birds now, Dr. S.," says Ciel after a moment, recovering their composure with a bit of a laugh, "then consider me suitably impressed—but was calling me an 'astrophysicist' really too much of a stretch for her to learn?"

Bernadette tilts her head to one side and considers this, then turns back to Mother and flaps her wings to draw attention to the correction she apparently needs to make. "Ciel-is-impressed-astrophysicist!"

"Very good, Bernie!" says Mother. "Do you know what that means?"

"Star-doctor!" Bernadette replies, quite pleased with herself. Coby had explained to her once in one of their one-sided conversations that the person they talked about called Ciel was, in addition to their main line of work, a scientist like Mother who studied big important things called *stars* instead of creatures, but they hadn't told her what Ciel's job was called. She's happy to know that there's a proper word for it.

Freiburg's eyes widen. "Okay, Dr. S., this has to be one of your more involved magic tricks. How did you know to train her for prompts like that?"

"Believe it or not, I didn't teach her to say any of it." Mother chuckles and takes out her holoscreen to make some more notes. "Bernie," she asks, gesturing with her stylus, "can you tell the Lieutenants the phrases Coby and I were trying to teach you and Albert to say?"

Bernadette chirps happily and bobs her head before beginning her recitation. "Bernadette-is-a-good-budgie! Bird-at-work! All-clear-all-clear! Danger-move-away!"

"Thank you, Bernie, just like that." Mother smiles and looks back to Ciel and Freiburg. "You see, we had just started with a few phrases that I'd planned to later try to have her associate with tasks and the presence or absence of miasmas, if it turned out my theories were correct about her being able to sense them. The *rest* of her vocabulary she's either picked up from Rico or from the conversations she's overheard—as far as I know, just now is the first time anyone's said the word 'astrophysicist' around her."

"That's... well, it's outside my field—and bird intelligence is notable, of course—but even your little friend Rico doesn't seem to *understand* what he says," Ciel comments, looking at Bernadette intently and waving their tail. "And yet... your Bernadette here gives the impression she understands everything we're saying."

"That's essentially what Zoë said earlier, which is why I've been testing her—granted, *Cobalt's* been talking to Bernadette as if she could understand them since long before she started mimicking words." Mother sighs lightly and holds up a hand before anyone can comment. "Which, *yes*, I know, I talk to the birds all the time myself even though I'm well aware they can't understand... but I'm afraid I may have missed the significance of what was going on here because I mistook Cobalt's interactions with her for a combination of them having picked up that habit from me… and Bernie being something they'd latched onto as a way of coping with everything else they're working through."

"For what it's worth, Dr. S.," Ciel says in a bit of a more quiet tone, "their mind has seemed far less troubled since you took them under your metaphorical wing—even more so since this little experiment of yours hatched."

"I hope so." Mother's tone falls to match. "I've been doing my best to support them…"

"The kid actually *talks* now and can handle being in the Drive Bay for a full jump cycle without having a nervous breakdown. Considering what they were like when Navy first picked them up from the Academy at Kapteyn? That in itself is a miracle." Freiburg lightly strokes his beard for a moment. "Now as for the bird here? I can't claim to understand any of the science involved… but if it's just a matter of imitating words and you didn't teach her, how in the *stars* did she know who we are?"

"Do you want to try answering that one, Bernie?" asks Mother, returning to her usual interested-scientist voice.

Bernadette stretches and re-folds her wings. "Bernadette-is-a-smart-budgie!" she tells them, "Mother-talks-to-Coby! Florivan-pair-with-Navigator! Freiburg-is-Ciel's-Zoë!"

"By that," says Ciel, chuckling, "I take it you mean you overheard them talking about us here and there enough to know that *Venture* has two Nav/Quan teams and you've already met the only other Florivans on the ship… and then figured that Hans here must be my counterpart because we came in together?"

Bernadette bobs her head excitedly.

"So you're saying this bird has the same level of intelligence any one of us does?" Freiburg raises both eyebrows.

"I suspect she might—or something approaching it, at least," says Mother. "If Cobalt's to be believed, Bernie's been acting like she could understand spoken language since she got the last of her feathers... but she's only been holding a conversation like this with the mixed phrasing you've just seen since today, as far as I know—I'll have to ask them when they come in from the jump shift just how long she's been seeming to respond to them."

"Her use of language reminds me of kittens around the age where they're in between losing their fur and hitting that first major growth spurt—you know what I mean, Dr. S., right? When they've got a *general* understanding of what the people around them are saying, but they're still working out all of the proper phrases and words for things."

"That does sound about right, now that you mention it." Mother pauses thoughtfully. "I'll have to ask Navy to help me do some comparisons between Bernadette's development and brain patterns and that of Florivan kittens..."

"It'll be interesting to see how Navy reacts to this little development at all." Ciel leans back into a more comfortable-looking position and lightly draping their two left arms along the back of the couch and around Freiburg's shoulders, respectively. "Considering that you *almost* didn't manage to persuade them to let you continue the experiment after they found out what Cobalt was carrying through the Strange for you, I mean."

"They've met Bernie a few times... but yes, I have a feeling I'm in for a proper lecture from our dear Elder in residence about all of this." Mother shakes her head. "Not that I have any idea *how* the exposure to Quantum Space while she was developing would have done anything more than make her sensitive to the presence of miasmas—and I wasn't going to start testing her and Albert for that for a few more weeks, because she's been so much slower to develop since she hatched compared to the average budgie."

"*And* because I have to help Cobalt run those tests for you, since Zoë put their foot down about you being allowed to work with bottled miasma again—I remember." Ciel nods. "And your other subject isn't showing any of the same signs?"

"Albert-is-a-normal-bird!" says Bernadette, hoping that the way she fluffs out her feathers when she says this gets across the tone she wants, since her imitation voice can't accomplish the subtlety of tone that the tall people's can. Albert has told *her* that she's not a proper bird often enough that she feels it's only right for her to turn it around and call *him* normal.

Mother chuckles. "As far as I know, he is, yes—we'll still have to run those tests with both of them, but Albert's development has been perfectly normal and he hasn't picked up any of the phrases besides his name. For a budgie his age, that's not all that unusual, either. I would assume it takes a more extensive exposure to produce the effects we're seeing in Bernie... but I have a feeling that this little experiment of mine is never going to be able to be repeated for us to find out."

"Considering that you seem to have raised a sapient life form simply by exposing it to the Strange on a regular basis as an embryo..." Ciel shakes their head, gesturing vaguely with their tail. "Well, no, I can't imagine Navy would let you *ever* pull a stunt like this again—much less the rest of the Council when they find out about your results. My Nida's certainly not going to like it, I can tell you that much."

Mother nods and grows quiet for a moment or two, taking a long sip from her cup before looking back towards the couch. "And what do *you* think of it, Ciel? Honestly?"

"As a fellow scientist?" Ciel asks, with a mixture of curious and serious tones coloring their voice. "Or as a Florivan who's responsible for keeping you and the rest of the humans aboard this vessel *safe* from the dangers of the Strange when we're traveling through it?"

"Both, I suppose."

Ciel pauses for a few moments, lightly rubbing at their temples with their free upper hand. "I'm not sure. For one, I think this whole thing has been reckless, to a certain extent, even if you *have* been using the protocols we worked out—and that if it had been anyone in the galaxy but *you* who'd tried it, the Council would have demanded the experiments be stopped from the moment they caught word of it. You're *fortunate* that they've always trusted your reputation and good intentions, Dr. S., even without Navy vouching for you, you know?"

"I'm aware of that, yes..."

"And the *ethics* of ever allowing your work here to be repeated or—stars forbid—*built upon* by anyone else who doesn't share your background with us and why we have to limit the research into the Strange that we assist with, or your understanding of when things have gone too far... that's a mess I don't even want to think about." Ciel sighs and makes a vague gesture. "And it's more Navy's place to talk about that than mine anyway."

"I know what you mean, yes." Mother nods.

"But as far as the bird herself?" Ciel brightens and holds out one of their hands. "*That* I am sure of!"

Bernadette takes this as permission to fly over and land on their outstretched fingers. She flutters her wings for a moment after she lands and then looks up with a curious tilt of her head into the three golden eyes that are looking at her so intently.

"Miss Bernadette," Ciel says, smiling. "Scientist-me and Florivan-me both are utterly *fascinated* and think that you are a brilliant little creature that the Strange seems to have decided to give a chance at being a person. I'm not sure if you can understand this yet, but you're very lucky that Dr. S. is your parent and not someone else."

"Mother-is-a-good-human!" Bernadette chirps, although this whole conversation her new friend has been having with Mother is indeed well beyond her understanding. All the same, she's *thrilled* that they're actually addressing her like this.

"She is at that," Ciel agrees. They hold the hand that Bernadette is perched on closer to their counterpart. "Now, if you want to start picking up interesting phrases to add to your vocabulary? This is your man! He's a brilliant Navigator, of course, if I do say so myself," they add with a grin, "but he's also something of an avocational expert on ancient human literature. You wouldn't *believe* the sorts of words all of his books have in them."

"Cici, *really*. Don't go talking me up to be an expert, it's just a hobby..." Freiburg seems embarrassed, but only for a moment. "But if we're going to say that this bird is a person and part of our little Nav/Quan family? Then yes, I don't mind helping Dr. S. round out her education with some readings from the classics—although I'm not sure how much good teaching her Latin would do." He laughs, giving Bernadette a little nod.

Bernadette chirps happily and bobs her head at him in return, then flies back over to perch on Mother's shoulder.

Mother lightly strokes her feathers and then smiles at the two people on the couch. "So! You agree that she's showing enough signs of sapience, then?"

"I do," Ciel chuckles.

"We might as well ask *her* if she is, at this rate," quips Freiburg. "What do you say, Bernadette? Are you a sapient bird?"

Bernadette considers the question, then tilts her head to one side and nudges Mother's cheek. "What's-this?" she asks, uncertain of the word from what little context she's heard it in.

"If you're asking for a simple definition," says Mother, "let's go with sentient life form who is self-aware and can think and reason. A *person*, instead of just a particularly clever animal."

"Bernadette-is-a-sapient-bird!" she replies, proudly fluffing out her feathers and flapping her wings for emphasis.

"Yes," Mother says, laughing brightly, "I do believe you are."

★

Part 3: The Family

"WILL YOU JUST *HOLD STILL*, BERNIE?" Zoë laughs brightly. "I don't want to solder *you* instead of these micro-wires."

Ever since they all realized that Bernadette was, in fact, intelligent and *sapient* and able to carry on a proper conversation with them, the tall people in her flock have been treating her much like they do Navy's three silver kitten-floofs. Zoë in particular seems to have warmed up to her—in no small part because unlike the kittens, Bernadette isn't in the habit of borrowing their tools and hiding them in hard-to-reach places around the ship.

"Bernadette-be-still!" she promises, allowing Zoë to continue carefully connecting the tiny bits of circuitry on the collar they're setting up over her mantle and breast to match the two little bands that they'd already put around her legs. The whole collar is designed with small, carefully-arranged sections so that she can move them to preen the feathers underneath. It's secured across her upper back with an even finer band running under the base of her wings.

"Do you really think this will work, Zoë?" asks Coby, who's been assisting them with the procedure.

"Well, the theory's sound enough and *she's* smart enough to understand how to use it... so hopefully? Yes."

A few minutes later, everything is attached and the latest prototype of Bernadette's personal tech adaptations are finally on and ready to test.

"Okay, Bernie. That should do it! Now say something."

`"Hello, world! I am Salzar-Newman's Bernadette of` *`Venture`*`!"`

Zoë and Coby laugh.

"Oh, *really*, now, Bernie," Zoë says, still chuckling, "I know that's a classic programmer's phrase, but the name Ari's given you is three times longer than you are."

`"It was the name Mother put on my registry paperwork when I hatched,"` Bernadette replies with a punctuating chirp. `"It's` *`mine`* `and I'm keeping it."`

"You really *are* Ari's daughter, aren't you?" Zoë pats her on the head briefly to smooth her back feathers into place over the circuits connecting the sections of her collar. "You've certainly inherited enough of her personality."

`"I will take that as a compliment!"`

The tiny circuits continue to do their job perfectly, allowing Bernadette to speak with a voice that's less garbled and imitation-like and far easier to understand. That was the whole point of this, really, to make good use some of the same sorts of micro-circuitry that Zoë specialized in designing before they became Navy's Navigator. The small set of bird-sized accessories started out as a modified and patched-back together combination of an old pock-et-com and one of the fancy earpieces the Florivans wear when they're working in Quantum Space.

"So, Bernadette," Coby asks, "are you ready to try flying with this on?"

"Yes!" Bernadette accepts her sibling's assistance to get to a higher perch for takeoff and then stretches out her wings and flaps them experimentally for a few moments. "It doesn't feel nearly as heavy as the last one, Zoë," she comments excitedly, "thank you!"

The unexpected weight of the first version of Bernadette's gear had been enough that the all-important flight test had ended with her abruptly falling out of the air and Coby having to dive and catch her before she could injure herself crashing into the ground. This current set is the result of the twelfth round of modifications to the system. She's pleased already with the latest prototype, but it's all worthless if she can't fly properly.

With another moment to stretch her wings and sort out the minor differences from her usual center of gravity, Bernadette launches herself up into the air and makes a few experimental flights around the room. Within moments, she's zooming past the open viewport and the sea of stars beyond it with ease.

"Flight adjustments are working!" she says,

chirping excitedly in her own voice to go along with the computer-aided output of the thoughts she's wanting to express.

"Good!" Zoë tells her, applauding. "Now, come land and we'll test your interface with the computers."

Bernadette wheels around the room and gracefully lands on Zoë's outstretched arm.

"Okay, what first?"

"Try activating your holoscreen projection, I think. That's what's most likely to short out on us again."

Bernadette flexes her wings and then tucks them away and taps the appropriate place on her left foot's leg band. There's a small pinging sound, and then a holoscreen roughly the same size as herself appears hovering in front of her.

"Good! Now, see if you can get through the menus and send Ari a message."

"Okay!" Bernadette gestures at the screen with her wing and beak to move through the menus, then pecks the appropriate button when it appears so she can enter the message. A few moments later, she's tapped out a message:

```
Look, Mother! No sparking feathers
this time! -Bernie
```

She adds as an afterthought a picture of her face with Zoë and Coby looking over her shoulder, then pecks the appropriate button to send the message. Having done this, Bernadette looks up to Zoë, bobbing her head and chirping happily.

"This is *much* easier than trying to hold

a stylus in my beak! Thank you!"

"Anything to keep my stylus pens from getting beak-marks all over them," Zoë laughs. "All right, holoscreen checks out! Flick it back off and let's see if you're able to interface with the ship's systems." Zoë carries her over to the workroom's computer terminal and sets her down in front of it. "You should be able to voice-activate it. See if you can find your record now and pull it up on the screen."

Bernadette chirps her understanding and then taps the terminal's activation button with her right foot and looks up to the display screen. "Show personnel record for Bernadette Venture, please."

A few moments later, a bio file appears on the display, complete with her full name and a listing of her pending legal parentage. A photo of Bernadette is included in the file, as are her bio-identity statistics and a link to the record that Mother had filed with the Interstellar Budgerigar Breeder's Association when she was a hatchling. There's also a link to the 'declaration of recognition as a sapient being' documents which Mother and the ship's easily-flustered protocol officer have been trying to file for her along with the adoption paperwork.

"Good, good..." Zoë says. "See if it will let you in anywhere else, Bernie."

Bernadette taps the access button again. "Please show listing of systems and files I can access," she says, tilting her head to one side at the display screen. She knows the system doesn't actually understand her body language or politeness, but that doesn't do much to change the way she talks to it.

A short list including things like "personal messages"

and "official personnel record" pops up. At the bottom of this is an entry entitled "educational materials and assignments." Bernadette, ever the curious bird, gestures at the words with her wing.

"What's this one, Zoë?" she asks, making an appropriate gesture with her foot to open the file.

The display populates with an entirely new brightly colored interface filled with pictures and what seem to be lists of subjects and tasks.

"Ah! Well, now! Pending legal status or not, no daughter of *mine* is going to get away with being uneducated." Zoë grins at her. "I took the liberty of enrolling you in the same 'education for children on starships' system Navy always puts their kittens in once they're old enough to study like human children do. A lot of the initial lessons will probably be refreshers for you, considering how much you've already picked up… but it'll be a good place to start."

"Really? Oh, thank you, Zoë!" Bernadette flutters up to Zoë's shoulder and nuzzles affectionately against their cheek. "So I'm not eerie anymore?"

Zoë laughs and lightly strokes Bernadette's head feathers for a moment. "Oh, no, of course not. It was only eerie when I thought it was a coincidence, you know. As it is now, well… Ari and I never *planned* on having kids, but I couldn't ask for a better bird to call my daughter."

Bernadette nudges their cheek with her head again. "I like being part of your flock too, Zoë."

Zoë gives her head-feathers another gentle stroke of affectionate acknowledgment. "Just try to remember how much you like us when you get to the point where you're sick of doing homework," they tease.

"I will! And then I will pester you to help me study."

Zoë laughs brightly. "Deal."

"Looks like everything's working, then!" Coby chimes in. "Who knows, Bernadette? After you get through all of these kitten-school things and into advanced subjects, maybe you'll be able to come to the Academy on Earth with me."

Bernadette is excited by the thought. "That would be stellar! Do you think they'd let me?"

Coby grins. "Well, my Nida and their Navigator and his wife are all instructors at Earth... I'm *sure* we could find a way to get you in if they helped us."

Zoë shakes their head, giggling. "Now, Cobalt, if you say she's going to be your Navigator someday—"

"—I'm going to be a starship's *captain* someday!" Bernadette's excitement spills over into motion and sends her flying in happy circles around the room again.

Coby's ears twitch with amusement. "She's smart enough to be a Navigator, but no—Bernadette's going to be my *Captain*."

Zoë sets a hand over their face, halfway trying to hold back laughter. "You two have talked about this already, haven't you?"

"We *might* have." Coby looks back to them with a thoughtful twitch of their tail. "What's wrong with the idea of her being an officer, Zoë? Dr. S. did confirm that Bernadette can expect to have a human-like lifespan. Why not let her do something brilliant with it?"

Bernadette lands on Coby's shoulder and takes her

usual perch nestled slightly under their tickle-y strands of silver hair. She's quite keen to hear the answer to those questions herself.

Zoë shakes their head again and then smiles at the two of them. "Well... I look forward to seeing you with a starship of your own someday, Bernie. But let's worry about fine-tuning your com bands first, okay? I want to make sure *this* ship's doors know not to close on you and catch your tail-feathers again."

"That *would* be nice..."

★

A FEW WEEKS LATER, BERNADETTE IS RIDING ON Coby's shoulder as they make their way back to their quarters after the ship's nightly Quantum Space Transit cycle.

Bernadette has gotten into the habit of listening in on the intercom announcements whenever she wakes to the static-like sensation shimmering over her feathers that signals that the ship has finished one of its jumps and returned to Normal space. If she times it just right, she can usually manage to fly down and be perched on the moulding of the door opposite the one to the Drive Bay's antechamber in time to meet her sibling when they emerge at the end of their shift.

Tonight, Coby has been in the Drive Bay assisting Navy,

which means that *tomorrow*, Bernadette gets to spend the whole day with them. As a provisional apprentice, they're only required to assist Navy or Ciel so many nights in a row, and then they're given a free day to rest and work on their other studies.

The two of them have just finished their brief visit to the bird room to do their usual end-of-the-night chores—not the least of which is to make sure that Mother has remembered to keep track of time and send herself to her nest to sleep at a decent hour. Tonight, they were both pleased to find that she had. Since all is well in the land of the budgies, they now return to Coby's little cabin attached to the quarters Mother and Zoë share with Navy and their kittens.

The rest of the flock seems to have already gone off to their nest by the time Bernadette and Coby arrive.

Bernadette has never been sure *why* her sibling's nest is in a different room from everyone else, but she's been glad to have a perch in the corner of Coby's space now instead of spending her nights cooped up with the other budgies. The door is a nice touch, too, since the three kittens are a bit larger than her and can be entirely too curious and cuddly for their own good. Bernadette does like the small silver members of her flock, of course, but there are times when she's very glad she can fly faster than they can scamper.

When they reach Coby's room, Bernadette flutters over to her perch. Her sibling flops themself dramatically down onto the nest of blankets they sleep in.

"Well," Coby says, "*that* was a long day."

"Agreed." Bernadette begins to preen her feathers.

"How did your shift go?"

"It... went." Coby briefly lays their upper pair of hands over their eyes. "Ciel told me that I'm apparently going to be tested *again* next week to see if Navy can clear me to sign with the Academy at Earth when we make port there in a few months."

"That's good, though, isn't it?" Bernadette tilts her head to one side. Her sibling is using the tone of voice that usually means something is bothering them.

"...Yeah, it's good, I suppose."

They still sound far less excited than Bernadette would have expected. She can't help thinking of the idea of being a proper space service academy cadet as a terribly exciting thing to look forward to, herself.

"You're not looking forward to being done with your apprenticeship?"

Coby hesitates for a moment before they respond. "Well, the bioscience programs there are neat, at least... *especially* because Earth has such an amazing variety of native species to study... I'm just... sort of not looking forward to having to try to find a Navigator who can put up with me, that's all."

"Oh. I'm not sure I understand?"

"It's nothing, Bernadette." Coby kicks off their shoes, which land on the floor one after the other with a somewhat satisfying thud. "Just... you know I still have the problem about... being sure I'm only seeing the things that are really there? I *know* it's gotten better lately, especially since you've been around to double-check with when I've had the odd off day, but I still..." They trail off and sigh, rising from their nest reluctantly in search of the softer yellow-and-white striped outfit they wear instead of their apprentice's uniform when they're sleeping. "Well, I'll be living with my family once I get there. I'll be fine. Don't worry about it."

Bernadette is confused, but she's also a tired little bird and has something of an awareness that there are things her sibling doesn't like talking about, even with her.

"Okay, then." She fluffs out her feathers and settles into a comfortable spot on her perch to sleep. "I'm glad you'll have a flock to keep you company while you wait to find someone as nice as Zoë and Lt. Freiburg."

"Yeah... I suppose I just have to hope there *is* someone like them out there for me." Coby turns off the light and then returns to their nest and curls up into their usual little ball under the blankets. "Goodnight, Bernadette. Pleasant dreams."

"Goodnight, Coby," Bernadette replies.

After a few long silent minutes, a thought occurs to her. She activates the little light source Zoë had included in one of her leg bands and flies over to the nest to land on the blankets near her sibling's shoulder.

"Hmm?" Coby's ears twitch and they open their third eye to look at her. "Can't sleep?"

"No, nothing like that."

"What, then?"

"Well," she begins, hopping a little closer to their face, "Ciel told me before about how Florivans don't dream like humans do, but how some of you can sort of *share* that experience because it's on a similar wavelength to the way you sense Quantum Space…"

"Oh, did they?" Coby's voice takes on a curious lilt. "So, what's got you thinking about that now?"

"Well," she replies, gesturing with her wing, "we know that *I* experience dreams, and Mother and Navy did decide that a lot of my brainwave patterns look more similar to a human's than a 'normal' budgie's. I was wondering if that means you'd be able to get into my dreams too."

Coby seems to consider this for a moment, and then they raise all three of their eyebrows at her. "You know, Bernadette? I honestly don't know if it would work or not. It's been…" They pause, their ear twitches, and then they shake their head. "…Well. It's been a long time since I was a kitten sharing *Heather's* dreams, at any rate."

Bernadette notices the hesitation, but since they seem to be trying to stay away from the thoughts that make their ears twitch in that particular way, she decides not to call attention to it.

"Heather strikes me as the sort of human who has very *interesting* dreams." She's met Coby's older sister in calls over the relays a few times, now. Heather is a doctor and the best sort of an eccentric human just like Mother is. Bernadette is already looking forward to the day they meet in person.

"Oh, she certainly does." Coby laughs lightly. "I used to be just as good at getting into them as my Nida is, too, believe it or not—and they're one of the best there is at that."

"I usually have dreams about flying,"

Bernadette tells them. "And stars! They're nice. Would you like to make an experiment of it?"

"You know, little sister?" Coby smiles and reaches out to lightly stroke her recently-preened feathers. "I wouldn't mind that at all."

Bernadette chirps happily and turns off her little light, then settles into a comfortable position nestled into the space between her sibling's chin and shoulder.

It's not long before both she and Coby are fast asleep and the two of them are soaring together through the endless sky of stars where no other thoughts or troubles can reach them.

★

M SS *Venture's* first port of call upon entering Sol's planetary system is the Galileo Orbital Complex: a veritable metropolis of a space station floating on the outer edge of Saturn's rings. The largest such marvel of engineering and architecture yet built by humans, the Complex is the primary hub of activity for ships which travel between Earth and the system's outermost settlements, as well as one of the major stops for many interstellar voyages.

In the sitting area in her little family's quarters, Dr. Salzar-Newman is pacing back and forth across the full length of the space, muttering quietly to herself. The ship's three resident Florivan kittens, still mostly silver-furred, follow her in a remarkably orderly scampered line. The kittens' parent is currently in their own small chamber off of the main family space, changing out of their uniform and into their seldom-worn ceremonial robes in preparation for an upcoming session of the Florivan Council of Elders. Their Navigator, meanwhile, is sitting on the couch, reading over a lengthy document the ship's protocol officer has just delivered—this being the source of Dr. Salzar-Newman's impulse towards agitated pacing.

"So, then... I suppose we can cross *Saturn* off the list too." Zoë shakes her head. "Another round of forms and paperwork awaits us to try for Mars next?"

"I don't understand why this is so difficult!" Dr. Salzar-Newman lets out a groan of frustration. "I've gotten every officer on this *ship* to sign the affidavits by this point. What more do I have to do?"

"Well, love, I'm sure Lt. Timms will get it all sorted eventually. It's not every new-to-the-biz protocol officer who gets to be the one establishing a legal precedent, you know."

"*If* he can establish it! Granted, it's just as bad even trying to publish my research on the project—and yes, yes, I *know* that's all so heavily redacted at this point it might as well just be a big black box with 'no, really, I *swear* there was science involved...' written in the footnotes."

"Now, Ari..."

Dr. Salzar-Newman makes a sweeping dramatic gesture with both hands as she continues, "...'but it's *secret* science that no one will ever be allowed to repeat and you have to be cleared by the Florivan Elders to know any of the details! I *swear* I'm actually a good scientist... I kept notes... that I can't show anyone.' And then a picture of our sweet little Bernie holding a sign that says 'My mother is not a mad scientist! She takes *notes*.'"

Having said this, Dr. Salzar-Newman makes a disgusted face and flops down to the floor in an equally dramatic fashion, stretching out and staring up at the ceiling.

The three kittens take the opportunity to scamper up on top of her and sit on her chest as if they've just conquered an island for their territory. The kitten whose bare patches are the lightest-blue of the three nuzzles against her cheek with a commiserating sort of a trilling squeak.

Dr. Salzar-Newman sighs and occupies her nervous energy with giving the kittens some well-deserved cuddling.

"I *know* you're frustrated, love, but getting worked up about it isn't going to do you much good—or Bernie, for that matter." Zoë shakes her head and makes a small gesture as she sets down the datapad.

One of the kittens takes this as an invitation to come snuggle with her instead so they don't have to share a single pair of human hands with their littermates. They make a polite little squeak as they leap up into the Navigator's lap. Zoë obliges and sets about lightly stroking the kitten's head.

"I just... I want her to be *safe*, Zoë. I *know* what could happen if we can't get one of the planets to cooperate and grant her citizenship—and she deserves to be treated as a proper person, now that we know she is one." Dr. Salzar-Newman sighs, still staring up at the ceiling. "*Especially* since Bernie wants to do something more with her life than be *Venture's* little feathered curiosity."

"I have faith in you, Ari. You'll sort it out."

The door chimes.

"Enter," calls Zoë.

A grey-haired old man with an unusually large number of freckles comes in, Bernadette contentedly riding on his shoulder. This is *Venture's* Captain, one Gunther Hannemann. Since being formally introduced to the newest sapient life form on his ship, the man has developed a marked fondness for the bird, treating her more as a protégé than in the somewhat grandfatherly way he does Navy's kittens.

"Ah," says the Captain, eying Dr. Salzar-Newman's posture with no small amusement. "It seems your mother has received the news Lt. Timms mentioned to us, Miss Chirps."

Bernadette flies down to land on her forehead and looks curiously into her eyes. "Did the paperwork attack you again, Mother?"

"Oh, it *did*, Bernie... But don't worry, I'll be ready to tilt at windmills again tomorrow."

"Windmills?" repeats the turquoise-patched kitten sitting in Zoë's lap. They and their siblings have started to pick up words here and there now, although none of them have yet taken on full sentences.

"Well, that answers the question of what story I'm asking Hans to read the three of you the next time he's kitten-sitting!" says Zoë with a chuckle. "Have a seat if you like, Captain; Navy's still getting changed for their Council meeting."

"Ah, yes, that's today, isn't it? I feel like they said something about that earlier..." The old man takes a seat in one of the chairs near the couch and shakes his head, looking back down to the woman lying on the floor with two kittens curled up on her chest and a rather concerned-looking budgerigar perched on her forehead. "I've given Lt. Timms a few more of my strings from the old days he might be able to pull for you, Ariadne, but I don't know yet if anything will come of them."

"Oh?" Zoë raises an eyebrow. "And here I thought we were running out of favors to try calling in."

"You'd be *surprised* the people I know who've ended up in admin back on Mars," the Captain chuckles. "Besides, *Venture's* registered there—hopefully that'll be a point in our favor."

"I'm sorry all of this has become such a hassle," Bernadette says, stretching her wings and then flying up to perch on the little stand that's been added to the center of the coffee table for her.

"The hassle's worth it, Bernie," Dr. Salzar-Newman replies, still staring upwards and lightly stroking the kittens who have snuggled up together on top of her. "Don't worry about it."

At this point in the conversation, Navy emerges, dressed in several layers of flowing salmon-pink silk robes. A matching beaded headdress is set behind their large catlike ears with veils which hang down their back and obscure most of their intricately braided silver hair. They have beaded bangles glittering on each of their wrists, as well as an ornate necklace in the same style.

The kittens immediately take notice of their parent's reappearance, as well as the sparkle given off by their jewelry. They scamper over and hop up into Navy's arms to inspect the unfamiliar and fascinating outfit.

"Nida!" the three of them say one on top of the other

in between all of their other excited kitten-squeaking, *"Shiny!"*

"Yes, kittens," says Navy, laughing as they try to both catch and settle down the kittens who are climbing all over them, "I know I'm all shiny today—please don't undress me! I'll let you play with my bangles later once I'm done wearing them."

The three humans share a chuckle watching this. Bernadette, ever the clever bird, flies up to the top of the bookcase where she knows the kittens have a cache of toys. She pulls a particularly bright-colored ball out of the hiding place, picks it up with her beak, and shakes it. The small bell inside the woven cloth-and-wire cage of the ball jingles brightly.

"Look, kittens! I found a shiny thing! Come play with me!"

The kittens are scampering after the ball before Bernadette even finishes tossing it down from her perch. They happily take up their current favorite game: 'fetch the jingle ball and then chase the bird as she flies around the room carrying it until she drops it again'.

"Thank you, Bernadette." Navy laughs again at the sight and goes over to the couch to sit beside their Navigator. They smooth out their robes and look down at the floor, where the kittens are making a point of scampering around Dr. Salzar-Newman rather than over the top of her. "I see you're still in a dramatic mood, Ari?"

"Not really, but getting up takes too much effort." She half-raises her head off the floor to look at them. "You look nice, by the way. You should wear the silks more often."

"Thank you. I do like them, you know, but they're better suited to special occasions." Navy shakes their head. "Trying to run jumps dressed like this is just asking for trouble."

The Captain smiles fondly. "And here I remember when you were still complaining about your hair-ribbons getting in the way all the time..."

"Oh, now, don't go making us all feel *old*, Captain." Zoë laughs and reaches over to help Navy get the last of the bead strands in their headdress sorted out from having been rearranged by the kittens.

"That can't have been all that long ago, can it?" the old man asks.

"I was named an Elder five years after we joined your crew," Navy replies. "And these little ones are my third litter. It was a *while* ago, to say the least."

Before anyone responds, the door chimes again and then opens. Cobalt and Ciel walk in, each wearing a long silk tunic with embroidered sleeves and loose-cut trousers rather than their uniforms or usual sorts of casual clothing. Cobalt's outfit is shaded in amber, while Ciel's is in sunset yellow and includes a long tasseled shawl draped over their upper shoulders.

"Well, it took us a while to get sorted out, but here we are!" Ciel grins. "Lucky for Cobalt here, I *was* able to fix the sleeves to actually fit them in the end—although if they hit any more of a growth spurt, we'll have to see about getting them a new formal outfit altogether."

"I'll keep that in mind," says Navy, standing. "But you both look nice all cleaned up—remind me to take a picture once we're done with the Council to send to Cerulean."

"Will do!" Ciel nods and waves to Bernadette as she flies

past them, followed closely by the kittens. "Better pass that off to someone else, Bernadette—you wouldn't want to be late, now, would you?"

"Late?" Bernadette asks, changing course to deposit the ball in the Captain's outstretched hand so he can take up the task of kitten-distracting. That done, she flutters over and lands in her usual place on Cobalt's shoulder and tilts her head curiously at Ciel and Navy. "Late for what?"

"The Council has requested you," Navy answers.

"They have?"

"They *have*?" Dr. Salzar-Newman echoes. She sits up now, looking somewhat startled.

"They've all heard enough about Bernadette that they want to meet her. It's a *good* thing, Ariadne—trust me." Navy stops beside Dr. Salzar-Newman long enough to bend down and give her the same sort of reassuring pat on the head they so often give their kittens and then heads for the door. "I'll ping you all when the session's over."

Ciel and Cobalt follow them out into the corridor, Bernadette still perched on her sibling's shoulder.

"Well, now," says the Captain after the door closes, pausing to toss the ball for the kittens to chase and retrieve. "*That's* what I'd call an interesting development."

"It is," says Zoë, "and if Navy's not even mentioned it to *me* before now, it must be something particularly interesting that they're scheming."

"If nothing else, they're probably going to bring her back with one of the Eldest's lectures on personal safety to recite for me." Dr. Salzar-Newman sighs, but in a half-joking manner.

"I didn't realize they still did that every time Navy attended a meeting." The Captain raises an eyebrow, then turns his attention to the lavender-patched kitten who's just won the race to fetch the ball back to him to praise them appropriately before tossing it back to the other side of the room.

"Not *every* time... although since I started Bernadette's project, they've been checking in more often than they used to."

"They *do* care about you, you know, love," Zoë says, patting the seat on the couch beside her. "Now, what say you come up off of the floor before the kittens trample you?"

"It's a *comfortable* floor," Dr. Salzar-Newman replies in mock protest. After a momentary exchange of amused looks with her spouse, she laughs and moves to the offered seat.

Zoë sets an arm around her, then looks to the Captain and raises an eyebrow. "So, sir," she asks, "what sort of Martian strings did you say you were trying to pull? I know you well enough to know you've got a story to go with them that you're just *waiting* to have a chance to tell us."

The old man laughs, still at his game of kitten-fetch. "Am I really that predictable?"

"It's a good sort of predictable," says Zoë. "And the kittens usually fall asleep when we tell them stories, so..."

"So you'd be obliged if I got the little darlings to think it's nap-time so you don't wind up having to chase them all over the ship until Navy gets back to settle them, naturally?"

"Naturally."

"It would be a good distraction for all of us," Dr. Salzar-Newman admits.

"Well, then! Who am *I* to say no to a chance to spin tales for my smallest crew members?" The Captain grins and makes himself comfortable, tossing the ball back and forth between his hands a few times to entice the kittens to come up onto the armrests of his chair. "So, back when I first started piloting desert-racers at Hellas Planitia..."

★

"Now, Bernadette," says Navy, "do you remember what I taught you about being polite when it's time for the Council to meet you?"

"Yes, Navy, I remember." Bernadette nods from her perch on Coby's shoulder. They've told her all of the protocols for how to address people and behave in front of the gathering of Florivan Elders at least five times now—although granted, Navy has mainly been trying to teach the *kittens* all of that, since the three of them will soon have lost enough of their soft coating of silver fur to be presented to the Elders themselves and given their 'public' names.

"Good. They all already know about you, of course, but I'd like you to make a good impression."

"Bernadette makes a good impression on just about everyone, though," Coby points out, absently adjusting the sleeves on their tunic. They've seemed nervous ever since Navy first said that they'd be coming to this meeting too, although Bernadette hasn't had a chance to ask them why.

"Ah! And here's your first chance to prove it, too, Bernadette!" says Ciel quietly, flicking their ears towards the door of the small conference room the four of them have been waiting in.

A Florivan dressed in robes like Navy's enters, walking with the aid of a deeply carved wooden cane. They're a very pale greenish blue color under all of the layers of amber, and have some sort of dark protective lens band wrapped around their face which completely hides their lower two eyes and another lighter-shaded round lens over the third one. Bernadette's own keen eyes pick out the traces of scars peeking out from beneath the various lenses, even though the combination of the Florivan's skin tone and silver stripe patterning would likely make it more difficult for anyone else to spot these from a distance.

"Ah!" says the new Florivan with a wide smile, "I managed not to be the last one here after all!"

"Guirmean just sent me a ping that they're running late because two of their kittens found their way into *Tenacity's* aft hydroponics bay and still haven't been coaxed out of hiding—they said they'll be here when they get here, but that there's no need to make the rest of the Council wait." Navy chuckles knowingly and approaches the newcomer, exchanging a warm embrace with them. "It's good to see you, though, old friend, and not just as a relay-hologram."

"Likewise, Navy—it's been too long! I'm glad there's even three of us going to be in the same room physically for this... I spend *far* too many of these meetings all cooped up by myself listening to the proceedings in my quarters, anymore." They sigh in a way that sounds faraway for a moment, and then pitch their voice similarly. "And to think I spent so much time when I was Youngest complaining about spending all of my time in a Council Hall full of people..."

"You've said." Navy gives one of the other Florivan's hands a squeeze as the hug ends. "But what was it you used to tell me when I was first named an Elder? 'We survive, and thus we have meetings'?"

The other Florivan chuckles and nods. "Something like that, yes." They turn to Ciel now. "And goodness, it's been years since I've encountered *you* in person, too, Ciel—not since you were a little fuzzy thing and Cloud was presenting you and your littermates, at least!"

Ciel laughs and also exchanges a hug with the new Florivan. "And then your and Nida's Navigators had to chase the five of us all over Luna Orbital because we escaped from them while y'all were busy with the rest of the Council meeting. I remember the story."

Bernadette has come to the conclusion that this must be one of the Elders Navy had mentioned would be joining them, although since they hadn't mentioned any names she's not sure which one.

The amber-robed Elder reaches up and ruffles Ciel's hair, then turns and comes over to Coby and Bernadette. "I'm glad to hear you're doing well, Mereday," they say, making no move to hug Bernadette's sibling the way they had Navy and Ciel. "I've been worried for you."

"I'm... better, now, Ai-Nida—and I'm sorry I wasn't able to talk to you before for so long." Coby hesitates, then extends one of their upper hands to the Elder. "I did *want* to, I just..."

"I think I understand, Mereday." The Elder takes Coby's hand lightly in their own upper pair for a moment and pats it gently before letting go. "I'd like a chance to spend some time with you while both our ships are in the same place for once, though, if you're up for that. No talk of the past required unless you want to drag out bits of mine."

Coby smiles and gives them a bit of a nod. "I'd like that, Ai-Nida."

The Elder nods in return and then tilts their head to one side and flips up the lens covering their third eye and focuses it towards Coby's shoulder, squinting for a moment. "And this lovely little person with the shiny feathers must be Miss Bernadette?"

"I am, Elder," Bernadette replies, bobbing her head politely. "It is my pleasure to meet you."

"Oh, likewise!" The Elder grins and flips the lens over their third eye back down. "I look forward to getting to know you as well." They hold out one of their upper hands to her.

Bernadette accepts the offered perch and does her best to land as gently on their wrist as she can.

"And although I'm sure someone told you who all you'd be meeting today, I do feel you deserve a proper introduction. I'm called Celadon Toreval—I'm the Elder whose line your friend Cobalt is part of. You don't have to use my title outside of the Council proceedings—although again, I'm sure Navy's explained to you how our etiquette works?"

"They have, Elder Celadon," Bernadette replies, "although no one mentioned I'd get to meet my sibling's *grandparent* in person today."

"Is that a fact?" Elder Celadon looks over to Navy with a half-chuckle.

"It must have slipped all of our minds at once, with the day we've had—but to be fair, Celadon, if we didn't become the first of our own lines upon being named as Elders, half the Council would fall under your household still."

"Yes... even though Lapis is the only one of you who had the dubious luck to grow up with *me* for a parent." Elder Celadon says this in a way that indicates it's part of a joke that they've had for a long time, although there's just the barest hint of sadness lurking underneath their wind-chime-toned voice.

A melody sounds from both Navy and Elder Celadon's pocket-coms at the same time.

"Ah!" says Navy, "that'll be our cue to call in. Ciel, Cobalt, will you please take Bernadette and wait outside until we call for you?"

"Yes, Elder," says Ciel, with a nod and a formal tone.

Once the three of them are sitting on the bench outside the conference room door, Bernadette looks between Coby and Ciel with a curious tilt of her head. "I take it this is the part where we wait?"

"It is," Ciel replies. "Lucky for us, too—the Elders have a lot of formalities they have to go through at the beginning of an annual meeting like this where everyone's calling in over the relays at the same time instead of just the smaller portions meeting with the Eldest and Youngest for ordinary business." They pause, thoughtfully. "Well, *and* Elder Celadon—but that's mostly because they're still the Fleet's Elder even though they retired after the War and the other Elders like it better that they're always part of things."

Bernadette fluffs out her wing feathers and begins preening them. "So they're someone import-ant?" she asks, not certain of the context of everything Ciel is saying.

"Sort of," Coby replies, absently, "but they pretend that they're not most of the time because they like things better that way." They shrug and readjust the cuff of one of their tunic sleeves again.

"I will keep that in mind." Another question surfaces now. "And they're here alone? Even though both of you came with Navy?"

"Technically," Ciel answers, "the two of us are here for *you*, Bernadette. Normally Navy does all of their Council stuff alone, you know—and then they pass things on to us and to the various members of their line." They stifle a laugh. "It's a bit different for me, serving as Secondary on a ship with a resident Elder—most people only get their Council news from the head of their family; I get to have mine straight from Navy and then again when Nida gets around to calling me and letting me know the parts *they* think are important."

Bernadette now notices how quiet her sibling has got-ten. She reaches up with her beak to lightly tug at one of the stray strands of hair that's fallen out of the side braids they've attempted to tame the unevenly grown-out silver mop with and catch their attention.

"Hmm?"

"I meant to ask if there was a reason both of you got to come with me. I know the etiquette, but Navy didn't mention much about your roles."

"Ah, right. They've been doing the Elder thing all day and making a point of being secretive... Well, I'm here representing Dr. S. because I was involved with the experiment... and the committee Elder Navy's been talking to about you has already talked to *her* about what happened... and humans aren't allowed in full Council meetings like this one unless something really important is going on."

"And I'm here," Ciel adds, "because Navy has to stand as the Elder overseeing this situation and Cobalt here isn't an adult yet—and *someone* has to present you."

"I suppose that does make sense."

"I'm just glad I'm not the one all of the Elders are gossiping about anymore," Coby says, barely more than a whisper.

Ciel gives them a particularly knowing look. "I'm also here for *you* today, if you need me."

"...I know. Thank you."

Bernadette doesn't know what the two of them are talking about, but she assumes it's something to do with the way her sibling sometimes gets overwhelmed with things—which means there's not much for her to say on the subject, so she settles for giving Coby's cool silver-striped cheek a little nudge with her head as a way of saying she is also there to support them.

★

It's a longer while than Bernadette expected before Navy comes to the door of the conference room to say that the Florivan Council of Elders is ready to talk to the three of them. She rides in on Ciel's shoulder, since they're the one serving as her 'presenter'—although she's still somewhat concerned about Coby and would much prefer to be on theirs because she knows her sibling tends to feel more comfortable when she's perched there.

All of the hologram projectors in the conference room are running now, creating a facsimile of tiered benches curving all around the far wall and up to the end of the table. Several dozen small translucent Florivan figures in robes similar to Navy's are arranged sitting in the tiers, while a larger pair of figures are shown in full-body form at the base of the tiers, standing on the far end of the table from where Navy and Elder Celadon are sitting. There's an empty chair beside Navy, presumably intended for the still-absent Elder Guirmean.

Cobalt and Ciel come to stand right at the head of the table between the two real Elders in the room. Both make respectful half-bows to the group of projected figures and then hold their upper hands clasped in front of their chests and lower pairs behind their backs. Bernadette settles for making a bow with her wings spread out before folding them back into their usual resting position.

One of the two larger projected figures gestures towards them and begins to speak with a very formal tone. *"The Council greets and recognizes you, Ciel Yrvi, kitten of our Elder Cloud Yaril—and also you, Cobalt Mereday, heart's-kitten of Cerulean Mirawynd and the line of our Elder Celadon Toreval."*

"Cobalt and I thank the Council for welcoming us, Eldest," Ciel replies with a polite nod of their head. "We are honored to stand among you."

Coby nods as well, although they remain silent.

"Your testimonies in the matter of the human Dr. Salzar-Newman's recent experiments have been received and discussed by the Council at length. Have either of you anything more to say to us?"

"Yes, Eldest," says Ciel, "we do."

"You may speak."

Ciel addresses the gathered Elders first, relating again how they had been consulted regarding safety standards for the later stages of Mother's now-abandoned experiments after Bernadette fledged, but had otherwise been uninvolved in the project—and more importantly, of their firm belief that Bernadette herself is a sapient bird and how they had come to learn that.

Coby is next, and while Bernadette can hear the undercurrent of nervousness in their voice, they don't hesitate at all while they're explaining that they still believe Mother's research was underpinned by good intentions and theories and that they were and are happy to be her assistant even though the results of her work turned out so vastly different from what anyone had expected.

Once both of them have finished talking, the Eldest stands from their little holographic chair again.

"The Council thanks you both for your statements. Now, as a resolution on this situation: Based on the submitted testimonies of all concerned and on the recommendation of the Elders who have overseen the discussion of the matter, the Council is now resolved that while the result of these experiments is remarkable, it is neither possible nor safe for us to allow them or any similar research to continue. Cobalt Mereday, we ask that you please relay this with the Council's regards to our friend Dr. Salzar-Newman."

"I understand, Eldest, thank you." Cobalt replies, keeping a level tone in their voice and making another small half-bow.

"Our Elder Navy Irleeim has informed us that you also seek to make a presentation to us, Ciel Yrvi?" asks the Eldest, taking on a curious tone underneath their air of formality.

"I do, Eldest, yes." Ciel holds their hand up so that Bernadette can flutter over to it and be held out for the recording devices to capture and project properly to all of the various Elders wherever they happen to be.

Bernadette spreads her wings out fully and makes a deeper bow before folding them back again.

"This is the feathered person known to me as Salzar-Newman's Bernadette of the starship MSS *Venture*," Ciel says, with a more formal tone of voice even than they'd used when giving their statement earlier. "I stand before you to present her to the Council of our Elders as a fellow child of the Strange, that her name may be known and remembered among our people."

There's a slight murmur that runs among the smaller holographic elders, and then the Eldest nods and taps the walking stick they're holding on the ground twice, silencing everyone.

"The Council recognizes you, Salzar-Newman's Bernadette. To whose line do you belong?"

Bernadette glances back briefly to her sibling, and then to Navy, who's sharing a look of some kind that she doesn't understand with Elder Celadon. She takes this to mean that none of them expected her to be asked this question either, so she does her best to come up with an appropriate answer based on what she's listened to Navy try to teach their kittens.

"I am the chosen daughter of Dr. Ariadne Salzar-Newman and Zoë, who is Elder Navy's Navigator," Bernadette says, and then gestures with one wing behind her. "And from my hatching, Cobalt Mereday has been my heart's-sibling." Bernadette pauses and tilts her head lightly to one side at the little holographic Florivan standing in front of her. "Is that sufficient, Eldest? I do know the names of my bird lineage, if the

Council wishes to hear them, but they are
not of my flock or my family."

The old Florivan stifles a chuckle and nods. *"It is not
a traditional answer, Salzar-Newman's Bernadette, but the
Council accepts and will remember your line placement as
you have named it. Whatever else we may feel individually
regarding your origins, please understand that we are all
agreed that you are welcome among us as a fellow child born
of the Strange."*

"Thank you, Eldest," Bernadette says, bobbing
her head politely. "I am grateful to exist and
be welcomed."

This, in the end, is it; soon Bernadette, Ciel, and Cobalt
are all once again outside the conference room.

"Well, now," Ciel says, grinning and stretching their
upper pair of arms, "that went even more smoothly than
I expected! Congratulations, Bernadette, it looks like the
Council liked you."

"That's good!" Bernadette preens an errant feather
underneath her collar.

"You were lucky," Coby tells her, finally seeming to relax.
"When kittens get presented and receive their public names,
they have to recite as many of their ancestors in order as
their parent's been able to get them to memorize—and at
the age where we get presented, most of us are still having
to learn how *sentences* work in the first place."

"Which is more of a formality, of course, and they get
a bit of coaching if they need it." Ciel shakes their head.
"Although I didn't think they'd ask *you*, Bernadette—but
you got the answer right anyway! At least, you got it as
close as someone who isn't Florivan could answer."

"I'm glad you think so." Bernadette flutters her wings proudly. "Thank you both for coming with me."

"So," says Ciel, "we have a few hours now most likely before the Elders are done with their business... there's a nice café here on the station near a balcony that overlooks the main plaza level—what say we ping the Navigators to come join us for some triumphant snacks while we wait?"

"And Mother and the kittens?" asks Bernadette, flicking out her personal holoscreen to start tapping out the messages.

"Naturally!" Ciel laughs and leads the way down the appropriate corridor. "This is a *family* triumph day, after all."

★

L ATER THAT DAY, BERNADETTE FINDS HERSELF perched in the middle of a pair of pushed-together tables near the balcony Ciel had mentioned, surrounded by all of her favorite people. The three human members of her flock had come to join them soon after they first reached the café, and now Navy has finally arrived to complete the set and take custody back of their offspring. The other two Elders have joined the group as well while they wait for their own Navigators to appear from whatever errands they've been running elsewhere on the station.

"So," asks Zoë, sipping her coffee slowly now that she's no longer having to focus on keeping overly-curious kittens out of it, "did the Council meeting go well, then?"

"Better than usual, believe it or not." Navy shares a

conspiratorial sort of expression with Elders Celadon and Guirmean.

"Miss Bernadette's presentation went well, too, as far as the Council is concerned," adds Elder Guirmean, gesturing with one of their upper pair of deep-indigo-shaded hands. "I'm a bit disappointed still that I wasn't able to be there for that, of course—but I heard *nothing* but good things about it."

"I knew they'd like you, Bernie!" Mother maintains her triumphant mood, although it's clearly tempered a bit by the news she'd received earlier. "Now, all we have to do is get a single planet to actually *accept* all of the paperwork we've been trying to file and grant you citizenship so that you're acknowledged as a person under human laws..."

"Don't let yourself worry too much, Ariadne," says Elder Celadon with a practiced cryptic tone, gesturing back towards the café entrance. "I doubt you'll have to wait that long. That's your Captain and his protocol officer now, isn't it, Navy? Or has it been too long since I've spoken to the man and my ears are deceiving me?"

"Oh?" Navy looks up from the trio of energetic little silver-furred creatures they're trying to settle down and towards to the two approaching figures. They nod. "No, you're right, Celadon, that's him. My Captain does have a *remarkable* sense of timing, doesn't he?"

Once the two men have made the appropriate round of greetings and introductions, the Captain looks curiously to Navy. "So, pleasantries and promises of the best coffee on the station aside, your ping mentioned you needed us as witnesses—but I'll admit I'm intrigued as to what might have gone on with the rest of your Elders that you need any."

"It's less what happened than what's about to happen, Captain Hannemann," says Elder Celadon with a hint of a wry smile. "Which is part of why Guirmean and I are here too, aside from the pleasant company."

All of the humans take on the same sort of perplexedly curious look. Even Bernadette has no idea what they're talking about now.

"I do believe the time is right at that, Navy," says Elder Guirmean, looking around at the other tables. "There's a good number of people about who aren't part of our group and can be 'public witnesses' now too."

Navy nods and gets up from their chair, passing their kittens to Zoë and then smoothing out and readjusting their robes. That done, they take on an even more smoothly elegant posture than usual, now looking every bit as impressive and official standing there as the little hologram of the Eldest had.

"Bernadette," Navy says, holding out both of their upper hands together like a platform. "Would you join me here for a moment?"

Bernadette, ever the curious bird, flutters over and lands on their hands. "Yes, Navy?"

"Having consulted the rest of our Council of Elders," Navy begins, taking on their most formal voice and pitching it in such a way that anyone nearby could likely hear and understand what they're saying, "and in accordance with the determinations they have made regarding you, Salzar-Newman's Bernadette of the starship *Venture*, child of the Strange, and by my own choosing..." Navy lifts their hands to raise her up and gently presses their forehead to

Bernadette's own. "...I mark you now in the presence of these witnesses and before any who would have reason to know as a member of my household and a chosen daughter of my line, that any of my people who meet you may know that you have a place among us."

For the barest fraction of a moment, Bernadette thinks she feels the familiar static-like sensation of all of her feathers being ruffled at once, and then it's gone.

When Navy lowers her back down so she can look them in the eyes, they're smiling.

Bernadette isn't entirely sure what this bit of ceremony is truly about, but she understands that it means that Navy is wanting to be counted among her adoptive parents along with Mother and Zoë. Since they're being formal, she decides *she* needs to be formal too.

"Thank you, Elder Navy," Bernadette says, projecting her voice at a similar tone and volume to theirs. "I am *honored* to be so marked."

"Lovely!" says Elder Celadon, clapping lightly with both pairs of hands. "And now I have the delightful task of pinging the Eldest to let them know that everything is all official and can be passed on to our archivists."

Navy sits back down with a chuckle and lets Bernadette step back from their hands onto the table near the dish of fruits she'd been sharing with Mother. "And that's the end of me being official for the day! Do me a favor, though, Celadon? Forward the account of that to Lt. Timms here—I think it's *precisely* what he needed to add to Bernadette's files so we can be done with the sea of paperwork that's been drowning my household of late."

"I... think that'll cover it, yes." Lt. Timms looks even

more stunned than usual. "Forgive me if I may need to ask you later to help me parse how Florivan legal precedent interacts with coalition interstellar standards."

"And forgive *me*, old friend," says the Captain, sounding equal parts amused and curious, "but what does all of that mean? I don't think I've heard you use your 'Elder voice' like that since these two rascals of yours got hitched."

"It's pretty simple," Elder Guirmean explains, since Navy's taken that moment to sip from their tea and at the same time try to keep one of the kittens from accidentally knocking it out of their hands. "That's what a proper line-adoption looks like. As far as our Council is concerned, Miss Bernadette is legally a part of Navy's family now."

"And," Elder Celadon adds with an all-too-pleased grin, "between that and her having been presented to the Council formally... it makes Miss Bernadette here a Florivan citizen." They turn to Timms with a chuckle. "You'll find when you look through the precedents that our autonomy overrides anything that might be done under human law to claim she isn't anything but a person deserving of all the rights and protections any of us has."

Mother stands and comes over to Navy's side of the table and hugs them before anyone else can say something. "Thank you, Navy," she says, "*Really*. I don't know why none of us thought of that before... I didn't even know you *could* do that..."

"Well, Ari," Navy replies, patting Mother on the head the same way they do the kittens, "you've all been a bit focused on getting *human* authorities to recognize her— forgive me, but I'm a bit too impatient to wait while every planet in the seven systems has the chance to turn you down."

Bernadette, newly-minted "legal person" and "Florivan citizen" that she is, excitedly flies up to Navy's shoulder and affectionately nudges their cheek with her head.

"Oh, thank you!"

"You're welcome, Bernadette."

The three kittens take this moment to notice that Bernadette is perching in a place that's within their reach. They abandon their game of pestering Freiburg for bits of his croissant in favor of scampering over and up their parent's arms to join her on their shoulder.

"Chirps!" squeaks the most outgoing of the kittens, lightly wrapping both pairs of arms around Bernadette before she can think to fly away.

"Hello, Ilrel," Bernadette giggles, stretching out her wings to encourage the kitten to loosen their grip. "Please don't squeeze so tight. I *do* need to breathe, you know."

"Playtime, Chirps?" asks the second kitten, Irvai, also joining the hug enthusiastically.

"Oh, now, kittens," says Navy, laughing and gently nudging the two kittens off of her. "What have I told you about respecting poor Bernadette's personal space? She may be your big sister now, but you still can't all pile on top of her like this."

"Sister?" repeats Ilvin, who seems to be otherwise content with simply sitting next to Bernadette without trying to touch her, since they still haven't grown out of their mild fear of being pecked by anyone with feathers. They look up to their parent with the widest-eyed expression they can muster.

"*Sibling*," Navy replies, "but female." They tack on a gentle trilling chirrup sound onto the end of the explanation, as they often do when trying to teach words to the kittens.

The three kittens look to each other, and then between Bernadette and Navy. All at once, they start squeaking excitedly until they seem to come to some sort of a consensus.

"Shiny-sister!" the kittens say as a chorus, and then manage to hold themselves back from trying to hug her again in favor of one by one giving her an affectionate nuzzle.

"Just wait until you meet the rest of the family," Zoë quips, offering their hand as a perch for Bernadette to step to so she can escape the adorable smothering. "You've got *seven* older sibs too, but luckily they've all grown out of hugging people without permission for the most part."

"This flock is bigger than I thought!" Bernadette laughs and then flutters over to her usual perch on Coby's shoulder. She nudges their cheek with her head. "You're still my favorite sibling, though."

Coby smiles and reaches up to lightly stroke her feathers. "I didn't doubt that for a minute, Bernadette."

★

SEVERAL MONTHS LATER, THE YOUNG BUDGERIGAR commonly known as Bernadette Venture finds herself in one of the less crowded waiting areas of Earth's Lunar Orbital Complex near the airlock where the starship that has given her her surname is docked.

"Are you sure you remembered to pack everything?" Bernadette asks, perched on top of a duffel bag in the chair next to where Cobalt and her human parents are standing. "If you've left anything on the ship, the kittens might not let you have it back."

"I have everything that matters, Bernadette," Cobalt replies, chuckling. "You're just as bad when it comes to worrying about me as any of your parents, you know? I've lost count of how many times already I've been asked that today."

"Well, what can we say, Coby?" quips Dr. Salzar-Newman, ruffling her now-former assistant's hair. "We've all gotten pretty fond of having you around."

"We are," Zoë agrees. They smile. "You'll be missed, kid."

"Thank you," says Cobalt. "I'll miss all of you, too."

Bernadette flutters up and lands on Cobalt's shoulder. "You'll remember to send us all sorts of messages and pictures from the Academy, won't you?"

"Enough that you'll get sick of hearing from me, little sister." Cobalt pats the budgie's head with a touch of a laugh. "But you'll see me again soon enough! I'd wager it'll only take you a year or two to catch up and get in here for the Command track, the way you're speeding through your lessons."

"And *stars* help the Academy administration if they don't let her try," says Navy, finally returning from the talk they've been having in a nearby meeting room with Cobalt's parent and their Navigator, "because knowing my little feathered heart's-daughter, she's liable to find a way to sneak herself in anyway just to spite them for underestimating her."

"I would, too!" Bernadette agrees. "But it's more fun to try to earn a place on the Command track the same way a human student would."

"Well, now," says Cobalt's parent, Cerulean Mirawynd. They pick up the two duffel bags from the chair and hand them to their Navigator, a pale balding man with a salt-

and-sand beard known as Julian Potts. "We can leave just about anytime, since we have our own mini-shuttle to take down, courtesy of the Tactical Flight program... but I believe *Venture's* scheduled to depart in an hour?"

"They won't be leaving without us, Cerulean," Zoë comments with a light laugh. "At least, not if Hans and Cici know what's good for them and don't want to be kitten-sitting for the next six months."

"Your poor secondaries certainly don't deserve that! I've only ever had one little silver rascal to deal with at a time and it was practically impossible to keep *either* of them out of trouble for more than five minutes." Potts shakes his head sagely, doing his best not to laugh. His eyes glance meaningfully first to Cerulean and then to Cobalt. "I don't know how you do it, Navy."

"Parental instinct and a lot of practice, Julian." Navy chuckles. "And, thankfully, a ship full of people who like kittens enough to help me with them."

"That being said, we should probably let you get back to them." Cerulean nudges their Navigator with the tuft at the tip of their long prehensile tail and then looks back to Cobalt. "Are you ready to go, Coby?"

"I... yes, I think so, Nida," Cobalt nods, albeit with some reluctance coloring their voice. "I've been saying so many goodbyes lately, I'm kind of glad we waited for these until now."

The young soon-to-be cadet shares a brief but affectionate hand-squeeze as part of their exchange of goodbyes with both Navy and Zoë. When they come to Dr. Salzar-Newman, they start to do the same, then somewhat impulsively wrap all four of their arms around her in a genuine hug.

"Thank you," Cobalt whispers to her, "for... all the things, really. And for my little sister." After a long moment, they let go and stand a bit sheepishly there in front of her.

"Take care of yourself, Coby." Dr. Salzar-Newman reaches out one last time and ruffles the now-nearly-shoulder-length mess of Cobalt's silver hair. "You'll *always* have a place on my team waiting for you if you get sick of Academy formality."

Cobalt nods, and then gives the little bird still sitting on their shoulder a light stroking of her head-feathers. "I'll see you again soon, Bernadette," they say. "Okay?"

"You will!" Bernadette replies, "and I will miss you until then, Coby."

"And I you, little sister."

With that, soon both little families have parted ways: Cobalt's to make their way down to Earth and the Sol Central Space Service Academy to begin the next era of their life, and Bernadette's to the starship *Venture*, soon to depart on its next round of journeying between planets and stars.

And yet, as is often the case at such partings, the two oddly paired siblings have no doubt that their lives will someday take paths which will lead them back together.

★ **THE END** ★

Appendix

TIMELINE OF *STRANGE SPACE™ ADVENTURES*

The following timeline lists all of the published *Strange Space™ Adventures* and Short Stories in roughly chronological order. Where stories feature major time skips, they have been placed based on the earliest events of that story.

Short Stories marked with *[1] can be found in *Tales of the Navigators: Volume 1*.

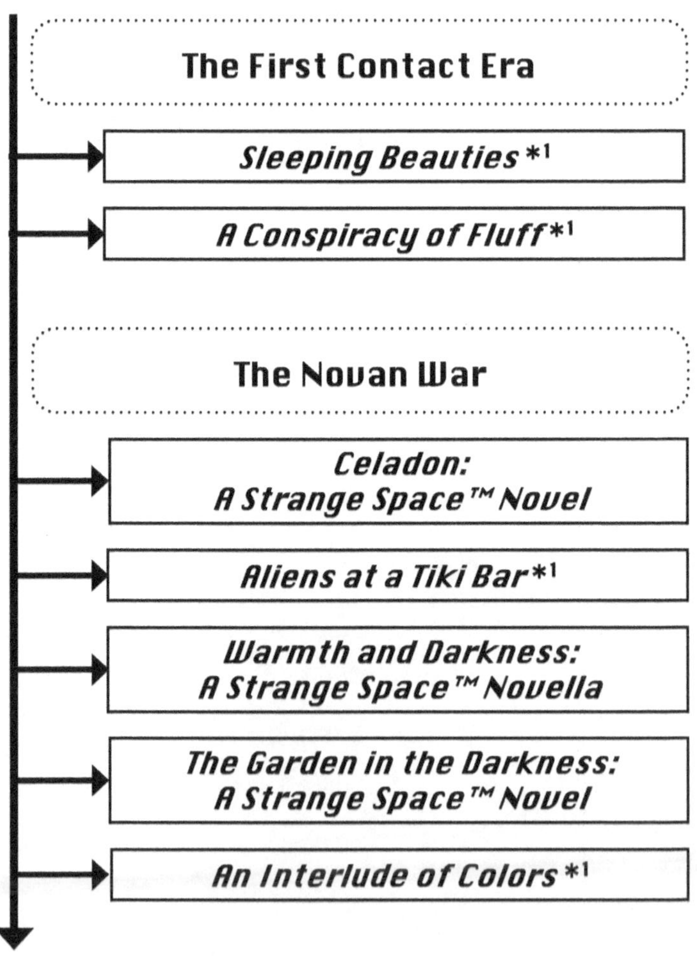

The Post-War Era

A Mystery, Unsolved [1]

The Ones who Wear White Hats [1]

Feathered Friendship:
A Strange Space™ Novella

On the Subject of
Kittens and Mittens:
A Strange Space™ Novella

The View from a Distance [1]

Fox in the Cave [1]

Rooftops and Space Whales [1]

How Ocean Merlani Stole their
Navigator:
A Strange Space™ Novel

The Tragedy of Harold the Violet [1]

On Character Identities and Pronouns

Feathered Friendship takes place in a far future setting in which human society has long since reached the stage of accepting and celebrating all varieties of diversity. This is a sort of world that I, personally, would like to live in. I don't claim it to be a *perfect* setting, but I do take an optimistic view of our potential as a species.

Several of the human characters presented in this story would, in today's terms, likely identify with one or more communities under the LGBTQIA+ umbrella. While the narrative of this story did not call for these characters to specifically state which labels they would use, and I like to imagine that a lot of who they are can be inferred through their interactions, as a member of the LGBTQIA+ community *myself*, I'm aware of the importance of clear representation. Seeing characters like ourselves in stories where they are valued for who they are and able to live without being marginalized for their nature is, in my opinion, *powerful*, and a big part of my philosophy as a writer.

Please note that at the same time, it is impossible to represent an entire community in the form of one character. My characters are simply themselves, and while they draw on my own experiences and those of people I know, they are not meant to be "perfect" renditions of one thing or another. Just like every human, their various identities are *aspects* of them, rather than the entirety of their personality.

That all being said, the following characters central to this story would like to "come out" to you and share this aspect of their lives:

Dr. Ariadne Salzar-Newman would describe herself as bisexual and bi-romantic.

Zoë would use the attraction terms sapphic and grey-asexual. Zoë is also genderfluid, specifically ranging between female, agender, and nonbinary. Zoë uses "she/her" and "they/them" pronouns interchangeably, but may prefer one or the other on any given day. To render this in stories where Zoë appears without being confusing for readers who may not be accustomed to multiple-pronoun usage, I have made an agreement with Zoë and the rest of the characters to alternate which set of pronouns is being used for them on each 'day' presented in the narrative.

On behalf of all of my characters, I'd like to thank you, dear reader, for being accepting of them and respecting their preferred sets of pronouns.

I hope that we all will one day live in a world like the one these characters inhabit, in which a person can openly be themself without fear. I do believe it's possible for us to get there, too; every small step we make in the right direction matters.

—Katie Silverwings

On Florivan Biology and Culture

The Florivans are a curious species by nature.

Roughly humanoid in form with silver-striped blue skin, a second pair of arms below the first, a long tufted prehensile tail, catlike ears at the top of a head crowned with silver hair, and a third golden eye above the first two in the center of the forehead: it's easy to see them both as "human-like" and "entirely alien" all at once.

In the time of *Feathered Friendship*, the Florivans have been friends with humanity for just over 150 years. They've been part of a fully integrated society for less than thirty, thanks to the destruction of their Sanctuary planet at Procyon at the end of the Novan War, but Florivans had been serving on human starships as part of Astral Navigator/Quantum Space Drive Engineer pairs from the beginning of the association between the two species.

Aside from the loss of all but a small fraction of their population during the Novan War, the biology of Florivans is the primary reason there are so few of them left in the galaxy. (In the time of *Feathered Friendship*, their population is still in the range of 2,000 adults at most.)

Florivans reproduce asexually, but only perhaps one in ten of them will ever undergo the metamorphosis to become a reproductive individual; everything about the process is shrouded in secrecy, as far as humans are concerned. What *is* known, though, by the humans who find themselves as close friends with a Florivan with a reason to tell them, is that even the Florivans themselves cannot control or predict just *who* will undergo the metamorphosis or when it will happen to them. Usually, the individual is between thirty-five and fifty Earth-Standard years old at the time of their metamorphosis.

It's also known that both the metamorphosis itself and the process of going physically into the Strange and "catching" a litter of kittens are potentially deadly. The families of reproductive individuals are very protective of them because of this, as is Florivan society as a whole. To that end, by the time of *Feathered Friendship*, a starship with a reproductive individual as one of its QSD Engineers will *always* have a second Nav/Quan team aboard.

Kittens are caught in litters of two to five, and start their lives as adorable silver-furred things about the size of a sugar glider. The Florivan parent carries their kittens in a pouch on their abdomen analogous to that of a kangaroo, although they aren't technically marsupials. The kittens grow to about the size of a red squirrel before they begin to mimic words and understand language. As kittens continue to grow, they shed their fur and reveal their unique shade of silver-striped blue skin. Around the same time they shed the last of their fur, Florivan kittens go through a series of growth spurts, after which they are similarly sized to human children and adolescents of the same age.

Florivan culture, in many ways, has developed around these quirks of their biology. The leaders of Florivan society are the Elders of the Council: reproductive individuals who have survived both the metamorphosis and the catching of their first two litters of kittens. An Elder's littermates, traditionally, become part of their household to assist with their kittens. The Elder's "line" then grows with each of their subsequent litters, as well as other non-reproductive individuals who are adopted into the household over time.

Florivan society is built around family and close friendship, and has always been peaceful—in no small part because they instinctively consider all other members of their species as close kin. A Florivan's human counterpart is considered a member of their family as well, usually along the level of connection as a sibling. Florivan Elders commonly adopt the counterparts of their adult kittens into their households. Traditionally, the compacted Florivan/human pair is treated as a family unit, similar to what humans would call a platonic partnership. Such pairs typically form after the Florivan has finished their QSD Engineer apprenticeship and remain together for life.

Another important aspect of Florivan culture when compared with humanity is their relationship to the very human concepts of gender, sexuality, and romance. To put it bluntly, Florivans by nature have no concept of these things. They are, without exception, genderless, asexual, and aromantic, to use the most accurate human terms.

(Florivans do, of course, find the vast diversity among their human friends fascinating! It's part of why they think humans are neat.)

In light of their genderless nature, Florivans are always referred to with singular "they/them" personal pronouns in English and whatever neutral equivalent is most appropriate in other human languages. They also exclusively use neutral terms such as "Nida" (parent) and "Entile" (parent's sibling) when referring to other members of their family.

On Florivan Names

Florivan names consist of two parts: the 'public' name and the 'personal' name. The 'personal' or 'kitten-name' is given to a Florivan when they first open their eyes, while the 'public' name is chosen for them when they are old enough to be presented to the Council of Elders. Some kittens receive one or the other half of their name in honor of one of their ancestors or entiles, which has become more common since the end of the Novan War.

Personal names come from the ancestral Florivan language, and are largely untranslatable. All of the kittens in a litter will usually be given names with the same or similar initial sounds.

Public names are always words from human languages which connect somehow to the individual's coloring. Kittens, therefore, receive their public names once they have shed enough of their fur to show a large patch of a recognizable color. Elders will often carry a theme through the public names of their kittens such as different stones, plants, or a specific language of origin.

Florivans are most often addressed by their public names. Only Elders, family members, or the closest of friends will address or talk about a Florivan by their personal name, and then only in private. (Private, in this case, also extends to situations where only other Florivans or close friends of the family are present.)

Florivans also commonly take on nicknames which are used by their families, friends, and colleagues. Who can use a certain nickname for them depends on the situation and origin of the nickname. Cobalt Mereday, for example, at the time of *Feathered Friendship,* is called 'Coby' only by their family and Dr. Salzar-Newman; Ciel Yrvi is called 'Cici' both by their Navigator and a majority of their colleagues and friends.

Florivan Elders are addressed formally with their title, although most of them will grant close friends and colleagues permission to address them by their public name alone outside of formal situations. Younger members of an Elder's line will call them 'Nida' ('Parent') or 'Ai-Nida' ('Grandparent') as appropriate in most situations. Apprentices to an Elder typically use their title as a sign of respect regardless of whose line they belong to, although the Elder may ask them to do otherwise in private.

Katie Silverwings is an award-winning author, glassblower, and artisan originally from Texas and now a nomadic creative spirit. She holds a BA in English and History from McMurry University in Abilene, Texas, with minors in Art, Arts Administration, and Biblical Greek Translation, as well as a BA (Hons.) in Glass from the University for the Creative Arts in the UK. Silverwings identifies as aromantic, asexual, and genderfae; "she/her", "they/them", and "fae/faer" pronouns are all welcome.

Long fascinated by nature and space, Silverwings' speculative fiction work centers around notions of optimistic futurism, friendship, found family, and adventurous journeys into the known and unknown. Her characters do most of the driving, and she does her best to keep up and negotiate pleasing stories with them.

Silverwings' two cats are commonly found staring over her shoulder while she's writing. The small cloud of dark matter with eyes likes to sit in her lap and interfere with typing, while the calico makes operatic editorial comments from across the room.

www.KatieSilverwings.com
@KatieSilverwings

More Books
by Katie Silverwings

Celadon

✦ A Strange Space™ Novel ✦

The Novan War has just begun. All that stands between Humanity and utter destruction are the ships of the Sol Coalition Defense Fleet.

The only problem? None of those ships are equipped with the all-important Quantum Space Drive which allows humanity to travel between planets and stars at a reasonable scale of time. The Drive needs Florivan QSD Engineers to run it, and Florivans are pacifists. Their Council of Elders has never allowed service on military vessels.

The Fleet can do little more than sit at the edges of the Coalition's seven member systems and *wait* for the Novans to attack.

Celadon Toreval is the Youngest of the Florivan Council of Elders. If anyone can come to Fleet Admiral Marvin's aid and help her save her people—and theirs—it's them.

Celadon, though, has their own reasons to get involved...

Available now from Amazon and Barnes & Noble and at
www.KatieSilverwings.com

Warmth and Darkness

The Garden in the Darkness

On the Subject of Kittens and Mittens

✦ A Strange Space™ Novella ✦

Ranger Captain Taimri Hämäläinen loved playing in the snow as a child. Now, on a vacation with her family in the snow-covered mountains of a certain planet in the Beta Centauri sytem, she has a chance to share all of her favorite winter games with her own children.

Taimri's three adopted Florivan kittens, of course, have never seen snow before; they live on a space station with her husband, George Barker. That only makes it more fun to dress Sky, Storm, and Ocean up in their warmest clothes and take them out into the frosted wonderland, in Taimri's opinion.

While her Florivan counterpart, River Myrval, stays behind in the cozy comforts of the lodge, Taimri and her kittens are in for a bit of an adventure they hadn't expected...